Venus Boy
60th Anniversary Revised Edition

By Lee Sutton

Revised by Lance Gentry
Illustrated by Richard Floethe
Introduction by Beth Sutton-Ramspeck

Text copyright © 2015 Lance C. Gentry.
All rights reserved.

All illustrations are the intellectual property of the Art Estate of Richard Floethe or of the Sutton family and are used with permission.

TERRAN
Published by Terran Press LLC.
ISBN: 0-692-58776-4
ISBN-13: 978-0-692-58776-8

About the Author: Lee Sutton (1916-1978)

My father wrote *Venus Boy* in the back yard of a small apartment in Gambier, Ohio, on an ancient Smith-Corona portable typewriter he set up on a card table under a tree. It was 1951.

Born in Redondo Beach, California, on September 24, 1916, he was named Homer Lee Sutton after the ancient Greek author of *The Odyssey* and *The Iliad*. He met his wife, Mildred, in 1937, and my brother Blake was born in 1943. During World War Two, my father was stationed with an Army Artillery unit in Italy, an experience that inspired both his first published poems and a distaste for violence that comes through in *Venus Boy*. Following the war, he completed an English literature degree at Kenyon College and then worked as a librarian and literature teacher. It was between his junior and senior years of college that he wrote *Venus Boy*. When I was born, shortly before the novel appeared, a family friend sent a telegram that said, "Congratulations on the birth of Venus Boy and Venus Girl."

When *Venus Boy* first appeared, science fiction for children was still unusual, but the book had many admirers. The magazine *Fantasy and Science Fiction* named it the best children's science fiction book of 1955. Judging from accounts our family has heard over the years, the novel also found many younger fans at their public libraries, where, it seems, the books were read until they fell apart.

Today, copies of the book are extremely rare, though our family has managed to find copies for all four grandchildren, who all love the book. Evan, the oldest grandson, now thirty-five, still has a teddy bear named Baba that has traveled with him in a backpack to Australia and everywhere else he has lived. Evan says, "He kept me safe and I kept him safe, and now he's my little girl's companion. Can't wait till she's old enough to read the book with me."

We're happy that with this new edition of *Venus Boy*, the book will once again be available to children everywhere, maybe even, some day, on another planet!

Beth Sutton-Ramspeck

Table of Contents

About the Author: Lee Sutton (1916-1978) i
A Hero of Venus 2
I. The First Two Secrets 3
II. The Treasure of Venus 10
III. A Dangerous Target 18
IV. The Third Secret 25
V. A Mystery Indeed! 34
VI. Inside New Plymouth Rock 45
VII. The Rhinosaur Stampede 53
VIII. One Secret is Revealed 65
IX. The Price of a Brother 70
X. Alone in the Jungle 80
XI. The Friends are Separated 95
XII. The Price of a Boy 105
XIII. Outwitting the Outlaws 114
XIV. Captured! 127
XV. A City in the Trees 137
XVI. The Thunder of Rhinosaur Hooves 151
XVII. Teachers Can't Play Hooky 167
Publisher's Afterword 173

"Everything that lives is Holy."
    OLD MARVA SAYING.

A Hero of Venus

If you ever make a trip to the green planet of Venus, the first thing you'll see will be the fifty-foot high statue of Venus' greatest hero. It stands on the very top of towering New Plymouth Rock at the edge of the old colony of New Plymouth. Even from the rocket landing pad, anyone can tell that the statue is of a twelve-year-old boy smiling up at the Venusian jewel bear perched on his shoulder. Cut into the huge rock below the statue are the words,

> "Virgil Dare (Johnny) Watson
> And the Marva, Baba.
> May their Friendship Endure!"

Virgil Dare Watson, called Johnny by his friends, was the first human being born on Venus. He was named after Virginia Dare, the first pioneer child born in North America, and for a long time he was the only child on all Venus. And that would have been a lonely thing to be if it had not been for Baba. Baba, the bear, was not only Johnny's pet, but his best friend, too, and the only one who knew about his three secrets.

Because of these secrets, Johnny got himself, his jewel bear, Baba, and the whole colony of New Plymouth into desperate trouble. And because of these secrets, he also became a hero worthy of a statue – Venus' greatest hero.

I. The First Two Secrets

It was Rocket Day on Venus! – the day the yearly rocket from Earth arrived, and it was like Christmas, the Fourth of July, and your birthday all rolled into one!

In the windowless, one-room New Plymouth school, Johnny Watson, a stocky twelve-year-old, sat toward the back of the room, a big Venus geography book propped up in front of him. Johnny was supposed to be studying. Every time Mrs. Hadley, the teacher, glanced his way, a page of the book slowly turned. The teacher was much too busy with the half dozen squirming, excited first graders to notice that a small black paw fastened to a furry blue arm was really turning the pages.

On Johnny's lap sat Baba, a perky-faced little blue bear with stand-up ears and bright blue eyes. To fool the teacher, the little bear, his eyes twinkling, flipped the pages one by one.

"We gotta do something quick, Baba!" Johnny whispered to his bouncing, jewel bear cub in a tight worried voice. "It's only two hours till school's out."

The little bear peered over at the clock on the wall.

He laid a tiny black paw on his blue button nose and cocked his head as if he were trying to tell the time.

When school was out everyone would go to the rocket field. Johnny knew that above all, he and his bouncing bear must not be there! Why Johnny and Baba dared not go was one of Johnny's three secrets.

There was only one thing to do, Johnny thought. He would have to behave so badly that as punishment he would be forbidden to go.

"Nudge me when Mrs. Hadley turns around," Johnny whispered. "We're gonna get out of here!"

The little bear shoved his furry blue snout around the geography and peered from behind it. His bright eyes followed every move the teacher made.

The instant Mrs. Hadley turned to write on the blackboard Baba gave the boy a kick. Johnny slipped down on to his hands and knees in the aisle and Baba hopped upon his back. Rapidly and silently Johnny crawled toward the armor room. Behind him a little girl kindergartner began to giggle.

"Look at the horsie!" she yelled.

Johnny heard the teacher call, "Quiet, children!" The little girl giggled louder. But he hadn't been seen! He scurried into the armor room.

As Johnny jumped to his feet and grabbed for his suit of rhinosaur-hide armor, Baba leaped toward the wall and hooked his claws into the concrete. Then he scurried straight up the wall like a fly and snatched up Johnny's helmet in his tiny black paws. While Johnny wriggled into the armor Baba fitted the helmet over the boy's blonde hair to encompass Johnny's head.

Without waiting to zip up, Johnny started toward the door. Baba jumped from the helmet shelf and landed on his shoulder with a smack. The boy's hand was scarcely on the latch when the teacher turned around, her mouth making an O of surprise. Quickly, Johnny jerked open the door and dashed through, slamming it closed. There was a space of a few feet and then another door. Holding the second door open, Johnny snapped tight his helmet, while Baba's small fingers pushed and pulled at the zippers fastening the armor. Both of them scanned the sky.

No arrow-birds.

Johnny grabbed a stone from beside the step and wedged it in the outer door so it could not close. To keep out these murderous creatures, all buildings were windowless and had double doors. When one door was open the other automatically locked. "Johnny, Johnny! You come right back in here!" a muffled voice called. Johnny sighed regretfully as he slipped out of the schoolhouse into the pearly green light of Venus.

Baba on his shoulder, he started out at a dead run through the collection of windowless buildings that made up colony headquarters. The two had barely made it to the foot of a tall heavily leafed tree when the door of the main headquarters building began to open.

"Up the meat tree!" Johnny yelled.

Baba leaped from Johnny's shoulder and rolled himself into a furry blue ball as he fell. The little bear smacked the ground with the sound of a bouncing basketball and bounced high into the air! At the top of his bounce his arms and legs shot out; he hooked his claws into the trunk half way up the meat tree. Baba wasn't called a bouncing bear for nothing!

Johnny jumped for the nearest branch. Weighed down by his arrow-bird armor, he was slow pulling himself up – too slow. Baba scurried down the trunk like a squirrel, his claws scattering bits of bark on Johnny. Hanging on with three paws he reached out and hooked his claws into Johnny's armor. One pull from that tiny but powerful arm and Johnny was sitting on the branch. From there up it was easy. The branches made a perfect ladder. Soon they were entirely surrounded by green shadowy leaves.

Johnny carefully pushed aside a green fruit the size of a cantaloupe and looked out. Striding across the dusty road came a tall man in helmet and black armor. It was Captain Thompson of the colony guard. The teacher must have phoned for help. The man's square face was set in anger as he kicked the rock away from the schoolhouse door. The teacher stepped out and Johnny could hear their angry voices.

After a moment Mrs. Hadley went back inside and the guard captain strode purposefully away toward Mayor Watson's office.

Sitting on a branch swinging his legs, Baba winked a shiny blue eye. He reached over and patted Johnny on the spot where the boy was likely to pay for his pranks.

"I think we've done it this time," Johnny whispered. "I hope it's not just another spanking." Johnny spoke with deep feeling. He had had three spankings in three days.

The little bear looked sadly down his blue muzzle and made an odd deep clicking noise in the back of his throat.

"Sure," Johnny said, as if answering the bear's clicks, "I want to go to the Rocket Day Festival, but we just can't."

The bear clicked again.

"I know," Johnny went on, "I know the Terrans would give you chocolate. Besides I was going to have a job." Johnny's eyes began to shine with tears he wouldn't let come. For the first time he would have been working on the rocket field with the men instead of being on the sidelines watching with the women and little kids.

The little bear patted him on the shoulder and clicked in low tones.

"All right, I won't be sad if you won't." Johnny shook the tears away and tried to make a joke. "Gosh, Baba, you talk funny since you know what." Johnny screwed up his face. "You're such a mushmouth now I can hardly understand what you say."

Baba stuck out his long blue tongue.

This was Johnny's first secret. His little bear could talk!

Baba's clicks were really the words of his own language. Although he couldn't make the sounds of the human voice, he could understand people perfectly. Johnny could both understand what the bear said and speak in the same clicking language.

This hadn't started out to be a secret at all. As a little boy, Johnny thought everyone knew that those clicks were Baba's words. When Baba came to live with him, the little bear cub already knew his own language, but Johnny was just learning to talk. He learned human words and click words at the same time, and thought everyone understood them. When he was almost five,

Johnny discovered to his amazement that no one understood Baba but him. He then went proudly spreading the news that he and his bear could talk together. When the first person laughed, Johnny didn't mind. But when everybody laughed at him he began to get a little mad. The crowning insult was being spanked for lying.

After that, Johnny decided if telling grownups that Baba could talk only got him punished and laughed at, it might as well be a secret. Besides, it was fun keeping it secret.

After a few minutes of waiting, Baba scurried along a branch and hung by his black claws while he thrust his blue button nose through the twigs and leaves. Johnny followed along another branch.

"Looks clear," Baba clicked. "Let's go!"

"Wait a minute." A quick movement in the distance caught Johnny's eye. Four men came out of a long grey building marked Hunters Hotel.

Johnny was instantly alert. Colonists always kept a sharp eye on such men. These were the dangerous marva hunters, whose only law was a blaster.

Johnny swung to a branch where he could see better.

"What's up?" Baba clicked.

"Hunters!" clicked Johnny. "They're watching the guard change at the old stockade."

"Oh."

The two looked at each other. Both knew what was in the stockade, locked away in the big safe. Marva teeth and claws. Jewel claws and teeth from grown-up bears just like the cub Baba!

"Come on, Baba." Johnny shinnied back to a place where branches forked from the trunk of the meat tree. "We'd better check your nails 'fore we go down."

After making sure no arrow-birds were feeding on the meat fruit, he undid one of his armor zippers and pulled a bottle of black liquid and a small brush from an inside pocket. Baba plopped down on his lap.

"Smile," Johnny commanded.

Baba pulled back his lips, showing black teeth. Johnny looked at them carefully, grunted, and then picked up one of the little bear's paws. All the nails seemed perfectly black, but on the tip of one of them there sparkled a point of bright blue.

"Dang it, we gotta find something better than this nail polish. A little climbing and it's all scraped off." Johnny scowled and dipped the little brush in the bottle of black liquid. Carefully he painted the tip of the claw. Looking over the little bear's paws he found four more claws that showed blue. He painted them too.

"Now don't climb down when we go, Baba! When the polish is dry, jump."

The little bear nodded.

This was Johnny's second secret. Everyone thought Baba still had his valueless black baby claws and teeth. But, under the coating of black nail polish, each of Baba's claws was really a precious blue jewel.

Johnny Watson owned a million-dollar pet!

II. The Treasure of Venus

Yes, a million dollars, maybe even more, and all for one little bear!

Johnny sighed shakily at the thought and hugged his bear to him.

"What's the matter, Johnny?" Baba clicked, waving his claws to dry them, like a lady getting ready for a party.

"You know," Johnny said, "I was just wishing for the good old days when you had your baby black nails and your pretty squeaky voice, and we didn't have to be afraid of anything."

"I'm sorry," Baba clicked. "I couldn't help it. I just grew." Baba looked so sorrowfully down his nose that Johnny laughed, swung the little bear up above his head and sat him down on a branch.

"You're silly," Johnny said. "I know you couldn't help it. I was just wishing."

Most of all he was wishing that bouncing bears didn't have jewels for claws at all. But he knew that was a silly wish too.

Grabbing a branch, Johnny swung himself back to a spot where he could see the hunters. As he watched, more were arriving. About a mile away a battered hunting tank came lumbering through the sliding doors of the fifty-foot high concrete wall surrounding the colony. Outside those walls, Johnny knew, lay the murderous animal life of the jungle planet.

Every living thing on Venus attacked men. Not just the huge rhinosaurs and the horned river snakes, but even tiny scarlet apes and pigmy antelope. Johnny knew the colonists and hunters would never have come to such a savage place at all without the lure of tremendous wealth to be made from bouncing bears' claws.

Harder than diamonds and just as clear, these magical jewels shone soft blue in the night and were blindingly bright in the sun. But that wasn't the only reason claws were valuable. A tiny piece of claw, or even of the duller teeth, melted in thousands of tons of plastic, made that plastic tough enough to be used for the hulls of rocket ships. Men called it marvaplast.

With such a treasure beckoning, man could not stay away from Venus. Rockets came hurtling across space filled with hunters. Traders followed. After the traders came the colonists, led by Johnny's father and mother.

Johnny sighed again.

"Don't be so sad," Baba clicked. "We've been real lucky so far."

"I suppose so." Johnny had to admit they'd both been lucky. Baba had been lucky not to be killed as his mother and brother had been. And Johnny had been lucky to get Baba at all. If there had been any other way of raising the bear until his black baby claws turned blue, Johnny never would have gotten him. All other young marva that had been captured had died. They refused to eat or drink.

They simply squatted down and whimpered piteously until they died of what seemed to be loneliness and heartbreak.

When Baba had been captured, Mrs. Watson brought him home, hoping to save his life. Two-year-old Virgil Dare, as Johnny was called then, was fascinated.

"Ba-ba," he had cried, trying to say bear, and had thrown his arms around it. Surprisingly, the little bear had stopped whimpering and had hugged Johnny back. A few minutes later it had eaten some diamond-wood nuts.

After a week, the colonists had decided that the little bear would live and he was taken away and put in a small diamond-wood cage for safe keeping. The little bear promptly refused to eat and almost died, whimpering over and over a sound that was just like "Johnny, Johnny, Johnny." It was the only sound he could make beside the clicking noise. He had to be sent back to the little boy. From then on Virgil Dare was called Johnny.

He and Baba went everywhere together, even to school. As the years went by they became closer than brothers and it was easier and easier to forget that the blue cub was really colony property.

Then, Baba's voice had deepened; the black nails had gradually loosened; and, all in one Venus night, during Baba's long sleep through five Earth days of darkness, the new nails had come in. Johnny had a mixture of india ink and nail polish all ready. It had worked for two months now. But the polish did chip off and the claws had to be painted over and over.

"Oh, Baba, why can't you be a sensible little bear and stay home where people can't see you," Johnny said.

"You know why, Johnny," Baba clicked. "You're my kikac." This was a word in the clicking language that meant friend, pet and brother, all in one. Baba said kikacs should never be parted.

That was the reason Johnny could not go to see the rocket come. If he went, Baba was sure to follow. Everyone, colonists and hunters, was going to be at the field, and if one of them caught sight of a flash of blue from Baba's claws, it would mean the end of Baba. The colonists liked the little bear but the colony was very poor. They wouldn't think long about killing him for his jewel claws. The hunters wouldn't think at all. They would steal him as quick as the flight of an arrow-bird.

It was a very dangerous situation. But if he could keep from going to the rocket field, Johnny had a plan. The plan depended on Johnny's third secret.

Draped over his branch, Johnny kept his eye on the hunters. They just seemed to be strolling about the settlement now – getting used to the fact that they were out of the dangerous jungle where they lived in concrete forts. When the door of the settlement headquarters opened again, Johnny pulled his head back in among the leaves.

A grey haired man with heavy eyebrows stepped out of the door. It was Jeb, the old hunter, one of the first men to come to Venus hunting marva. Now he was one of the colony guards, and a very good friend of Baba and Johnny.

When the old man came close enough for him to hear, Johnny crawled out where he could be seen, called down to him, and waved.

"Hi, Jeb. Whatcha doing?"

The old man stopped in his tracks, looked carefully around him, then cocked an eye up into the tree. He frowned, his grey eyebrows making a V over his deep-set eyes. He shook his head in disapproval, but said nothing until he was directly under the tree.

"What I'm doing isn't important," Jeb said in a gruff voice, looking up at Johnny. "But what are you doing up that tree when you're supposed to be doing book work?"

"Aw," Johnny started, "I just—"

"You just made your paw boiling mad, that's what," Jeb interrupted, "locking the teacher in that way." He snorted.

"Did Dad say anything about keeping me away from the rocket landing?" Johnny demanded anxiously.

"Nope," answered Jeb. "Cap'n Thompson wanted him to, but he says no, that you worked real hard all year. But I'm warning you. You better get on inside that school house, unless you want a good tannin'. Your ma's out looking for you with fire in her eye." He started to walk away.

"Hey, wait a minute Jeb," Johnny called.

"Well?"

"I was watching those hunters. They're sure interested in the stockade. You better tell Cap'n Thompson."

"We know they're interested. I don't think they'll do anything. That old reprobate Trader Harkness will keep 'em in line. You'd better watch out, though. I might tell Cap'n Thompson where he could find him a hooky-player." With a fierce snort the old man was on his way.

Johnny smiled. He knew Jeb would never tell where he was hiding, in spite of the gruff warnings. Jeb was a nice old fellow. He'd shot his marva years before, gone down to Earth, spent his millions in a few wild years and returned to Venus dead broke. In twenty years hunting he had never made another kill. Marva were as hard to find as they were valuable.

"Guess you just weren't quite bad enough!" Baba clicked to Johnny. "My claws are dry. Let's go before your mother finds us."

Johnny crawled down to the little bear.

"We gotta think of something else bad to do. It's that or just plain refuse to go. But then they'd think something was funny, sure as shooting!"

"There's lots of ripe meat fruit in the tree," Baba clicked, and grinned. "Maybe you could drop one on Captain Thompson!"

"Oh boy!" Johnny exclaimed in excitement. Then he frowned. "Aw, he probably won't come by here again."

"Somebody will!" Baba said. "Let's keep an eye out."

The two of them posted themselves in different parts of the tree and watched for possible targets for ripe meat fruit. No one seemed to want to walk under the tree. Finally Johnny caught sight of a short fat bald-headed man and a tall red-haired man leaving the Hunters Hotel together. One was Trader Harkness, who all but ran the colony, and the other, his bodyguard, Rick Saunders. They seemed to be headed for the trading post and would have to pass directly under Johnny's tree to get there. Baba saw them at the same time.

"How about Trader Harkness?" the little bear clicked. "Do you think he'd be a good target?"

"A kind of dangerous one," Johnny clicked back, his heart racing. "But where's that meat fruit?"

There wasn't any question about his getting into enough trouble this time. He just hoped he wouldn't get into too much trouble!

Trader Harkness was a very important man, but Johnny didn't like him. He had started as a hunter and then had turned trader. By killing off most of his opposition, he had become the only important trader on

Venus. If he hadn't wanted a walled settlement to protect his goods, the colony might have failed. A hunter would stop at nothing to get what he needed and the colony had had more than one of its tanks ambushed and stolen to hunt marva.

A red, ripe meat fruit was not hard to find. Johnny wrenched one from the branch and held it carefully by its long stem. The size of a small melon, green meat fruit must be cooked before eating. Once ripe, their thin skins are plump full of a sweet strong-smelling paste. It was a natural high protein baby food.

"There's plenty more," Johnny clicked softly. "Think we ought to get Rick, too?"

"He's too good a friend," Baba clicked back. "Besides he might not give me any more chocolate."

Johnny agreed with a laugh, and pushed leaves aside so he could see. He shivered. Below him came the most powerful man on Venus – a short, immensely fat man, who waddled forward rather than walked. On Earth he would have been laughed at, but on Venus he was feared and respected. He liked that respect and demanded it.

Johnny swallowed hard. The man he was going to drop the fruit on had once been ambushed by five hunters – none of them had survived.

III. A Dangerous Target

As the two men moved closer to Johnny's and Baba's meat tree, they appeared to be arguing about something. The trader glittered as he waddled forward. His armor was of the clearest, brightest marvaplast, and his fingers were studded with marva jewel rings. They stopped just a few feet away from the tree. Johnny could tell the trader was angry. Though he was keeping himself under tight control, his heavy jaw was set and his little black eyes flashed under his smooth, hairless brow.

"I'll put it to you straight, Rick," the trader's heavy voice rumbled up to Johnny. "I couldn't stay in business a year if I did as you asked me to."

The red-haired bodyguard was flushed. "Well, then, I guess I'll have to do it," he said in a tight, defiant voice. "If you won't warn the colonists, I will."

Harkness' jaw tightened. "Better think it over, Rick." His voice was still controlled and level. He gripped Rick's shoulder with a pudgy, jeweled hand. "Remember, those hunters trusted me. They figure my bodyguard wouldn't do anything I told him not to. If you warn the colonists, I'll have to make it clear you were on your own." His voice held a threat.

"What do you mean?" Rick demanded, pushing the hand from his shoulder.

"The least I would do would be to fire you back to Earth," he said ominously.

Johnny drew in his breath. He knew how much Rick wanted to stay on Venus. The trader got his bodyguards by paying their way to Venus. He agreed to stake them for hunting if they did good work for a year. Otherwise they were sent back to Earth. It was said that men who crossed Trader Harkness never made it alive.

"I'm sorry, Trader," Rick said, "but I'll take my chances. If you don't like what I do, I'll join the colony."

"I should have guessed it," the trader said contemptuously, "when you began hanging around that worthless Jeb." The trader paused and then the threat in his voice was no longer veiled. "Believe me, Saunders, join that colony and you'll regret it." The heavy man turned slowly and moved toward his trading post.

Fascinated, Johnny had all but forgotten the meat fruit in his hand. The trader was almost past him when he remembered. With a little toss Johnny let go of the juicy fruit. For an instant he thought he had thrown too far, but the trader waddled forward just right.

With a sickening plop the red fruit exploded on the top of Trader Harkness' shining helmet. Dripping purple gobs splattered through the air slits, smearing the stone-bald head. A strong sweet smell floated up to Johnny. For a moment Harkness stood perfectly still in shocked amazement.

Then the tremendous man began to dance about in sheer rage and discomfort.

"Water!" he yelled, his rumbling voice rising to a shrill cry. "Get some water!" He was bouncing up and down in an odd way, his clenched fists hitting the air. All his dignity was gone.

Johnny stared open-mouthed, awed by his own daring. Rick Saunders stood still a second, and then broke into a guffaw.

"I tell you, get me some water!" Trader Harkness roared. Three or four hunters and Jeb, the old guard, came running up. They took one look and they, too, broke into laughter. Jeb was carrying a fire bucket.

"Never thought I'd ever get this chance, Will," Jeb cackled, and sloshed a bucket of water over Harkness. The water splashed on the bald head and washed the bits of fruit down the trader's neck and under his armor. The big man stood there dumb with anger.

Johnny's throat ached with the laughs he'd kept back. He glanced up to the branch where Baba sat. The little bear's fur was shivering with fun. His eyes opened wide, and with a whir of clicks meaning, "Watch me, Johnny," he leaped into space. He kicked up a flurry of dust as he bounced to the ground and up to his feet in front of the trader and the other men. By this time the crowd had grown to a dozen men.

Baba stopped a moment to make sure everyone was watching him. Then the round little bear began a dancing, bouncing waddle up and down. He clenched his forepaws into little fists and beat the air. His face was screwed up into a mighty frown. It was a perfect imitation of the trader. The men's laughter swelled to a roar.

"Rick!" Harkness' voice rumbled out, tight and cold with rage. "Shoot it!"

The laughter stopped suddenly, almost as if it had been switched off. It had been so long since anyone had made fun of the trader that the man had lost his head.

"I can't do that!" Rick's lean brown face was horrified. Then he became angry. "I wouldn't shoot a kid's pet!"

"Well, I will!" Moving with more speed than it seemed a large man could muster, the trader's hand snaked toward his holster.

Baba saw the joke had gone too far. He leaped into the air, came down with a bounce and shot up the tree beside Johnny before the trader could level the gun at him.

Johnny's mouth went dry. Already the trader was searching the tree for Baba, his pistol up, the safety switch off. The men stood in shocked silence.

"He's right beside me, Mr. Harkness!" Johnny shouted, and crawled into full view. "C'mon, Baba, get on my shoulder. He can't shoot me." As Johnny came into full view, the trader's face grew angrier yet. "Baba didn't drop that meat fruit, Mr. Harkness," Johnny said firmly. "I did."

"Kid's got guts," one of the hunters muttered.

As Johnny slid down to the ground, he saw his mother pushing her way through the group of men. Her lips were tight together, her face white.

"You're going to get it," Baba clicked. "Here come your pa and Captain Thompson, too."

Mrs. Watson strode straight up to Trader Harkness, her eyes blazing.

21

"You ought to be ashamed!" she said to the man. Then she turned on Johnny. "And so had you, young man. No Rocket Day Festival for you!"

Johnny's heart leaped. He'd done it at last!

"Now, Mr. Harkness," Johnny's mother's voice was very low, "what Baba and Johnny did was very wrong. I apologize for them. And Johnny will certainly be punished. Nevertheless, I never want to hear of you or anyone else threatening Baba again. Is that clear?"

Taken aback, the trader nodded.

"That goes for the whole family, Mr. Harkness." Johnny's father stepped forward straight and tall and put his arm around his wife's shoulder. "Not to mention the colony," he went on. "We have a pretty big stake in that bear."

The fat, short trader seemed suddenly as cold as ice. His heavy jaw thrust out and his little black eyes looked straight at Johnny's father.

"Valuable or not, I don't have to put up with insults. Not from those two or any of you. If that's the kind of thanks I get for ten years of working with you, I'm through. You can fight your own battles now." He jerked his head around toward Rick. "C'mon!"

"I'm staying," the young man said.

"All right. Stay." The smooth bald head swiveled back to the Watson family. "I told this man I'd fire him back to Earth. But let him stay. After the hunters have picked your bones, I'll take care of him." He turned, and with heavy footsteps walked away. His slow waddle did not seem funny now. The hunters in the crowd stood for a moment, and then followed him.

Captain Thompson addressed Johnny's father. "That sounded like a declaration of war."

Johnny's father nodded grimly. "I think our colony is getting too big for him," he said slowly. "He's been looking for a way to break with us and Johnny gave him just the kind of excuse he needed."

"Yep," said Jeb. "But don't be too hard on Johnny. Maybe it's just as good it happened now when we got marva claws to buy us some extra firepower."

"You might not have those claws long enough to do any good," Rick Saunders cut in. "I was just going to warn you. Four hunters just asked Harkness in on a plan to rob the stockade. The trader turned them down, but—"

"Which four hunters?" Captain Thompson broke in.

A shadow passed over Rick's face. "I don't know which ones." He looked at Mr. Watson eagerly. "I want to help, though. I'm hoping you'll take me on as a guard."

"We can sure use you." Jeb stepped up and slapped the young man on the back.

Mr. Watson appeared to consider for a moment. He looked Rick up and down, and then glanced at Captain Thompson, who nodded.

"All right, Rick," he said. "You go on over to the guard barracks and Jeb will check you out. When you're through, report to Captain Thompson."

Rick Saunders grinned. Old Jeb threw an arm around his shoulder and they walked off together.

When they were out of hearing Captain Thompson turned to Johnny's father. "I don't know if I like this," he said. "Harkness may have planted that man on us. I'm certainly not going to let him get anywhere near our claws. I'll keep an eye on Saunders personally."

"But, gosh," Johnny broke in, "I heard him arguing with—"

"I think, Johnny," said his father sternly, "you've said and done enough for one day. The trader is a proud man and by making a fool of him you've given the colony a deadly enemy." He turned back to Captain Thompson. "We'd better change our plans, Captain. It looks like we should double, maybe even triple the guard…"

IV. The Third Secret

Three hours later, boy and bear were trudging through the marshberry fields toward New Plymouth Rock. Johnny's bottom was still warm from his recent session with a strap. The boy was in full armor. A leather harness was strapped to the little bear's furry blue back.

The last 'copter had long since left for the rocket field and, except for guards, the settlement was nearly empty. Because of this Johnny had been forbidden to leave his house. A lone person without a gun was supposed to be just what the arrow-birds were looking for. But Johnny wasn't afraid. He had his third secret.

Johnny reached up and carefully picked one of the apple-sized marshberries for himself. It was a rich ripe yellow color.

"They are just right this year," Johnny said to Baba.

The little bear nodded gravely. Both he and Johnny had worked hard in those fields. Everyone did. Marshberries prevented a disease called colds that Johnny had never had, and were the only crop the colonists could send back to Earth. They had to be ripe for the yearly rocket or a year's work was wasted.

Johnny trudged on under the weight of his armor while Baba bounced along beside him. A mile away loomed New Plymouth Rock. The huge mesa-like rock made up one corner of the settlement's barrier against the animals. The thick concrete walls of the settlement, topped with live wires, were joined to the rock on two sides. On its summit, stood a stunted diamond-wood tree. This was Johnny's and Baba's destination.

Baba jumped high in the air, made himself into a ball and bounded on ahead.

"Hurry up!" he clicked.

"Hungry for nuts, eh?" Johnny asked.

"Crunchy ones," the little bear clicked back, turning a somersault in the air. "Come on, hurry!"

Johnny made a face at Baba. "Bear," he said, "you're certainly getting bossy lately."

Baba did another somersault, bounced, and landed on Johnny's shoulder with a thump, almost knocking the boy down. He put his nose in Johnny's ear.

"I'm a grownup," he clicked in heavy tones. "Hear my beautiful new voice?"

Johnny hunched his shoulders hard, spilling Baba to the ground. Then he grabbed him by the harness, and stood up. While Baba squeaked piteously, Johnny swung him round and round. At the top of one of the swings he let go, tossing Baba high into the air.

"Help! Help!" clicked Baba, beating paws into the air, and screwing up his face. Just before he hit the ground he made himself into a ball. He hit with a smack and bounced higher than Johnny had thrown him. Both of them were laughing when he stopped bouncing.

"Gosh, I wish we could have done that for the Terrans!" Johnny said.

The two fell silent, both thinking of the fun they were missing at the rocket field.

They were coming to the end of the marshberry fields. Before them were the great boulders surrounding New Plymouth Rock. Johnny had made the harness Baba was wearing for forays among the boulders – forbidden forays, for arrow-birds nested there. Baba, with his strong nails and bouncy body, could go straight up the face of rocks. He was small enough to ride on Johnny's shoulder, but he was powerful too. By hanging on to Baba's harness, Johnny could go straight up and over large boulders, armor and all.

"Let's go right by the nests," Baba clicked. "I want to be sure, right off."

"O.K., worry bear, you lead the way." Johnny began to chant, "Grandpapa Baba sat in a corner, 'fraid that his shadow would burn in the fire."

Baba bounced over the smaller rocks in the way. Johnny, weighed down with helmet and armor, made his way slowly over them and between them. Baba helped Johnny over one steep place and then stayed beside him. It was hard going and Johnny's clothes were drenched with sweat under his armor before they clambered down the last boulder and on to a little flat place. They were already high above the level of the settlement. On one side they were surrounded by high red boulders. On the other side loomed the sheer cliff of New Plymouth Rock.

Far above them, from many round holes in the rock, came strange squeaking sounds. Here were the arrow-bird nests! Johnny was deathly afraid. He'd seen what an arrow-bird could do when it shot itself at a man.

"Get ready, Baba," he whispered.

"Those are just babies up there," Baba clicked. "No danger yet!"

"Let's climb up and get rid of them!" Johnny suggested. "Then there won't be any here to—"

"No!" Baba interrupted.

"But why? I'd be protected by my armor and—"

"No!" Baba clicked more firmly. There was a stern but puzzled expression on the little bear's face. "The arrow-birds are my friend-pets, I must not hurt them." He used a word in the clicking language which meant both friend and pet. It was something like the word "kikac," which he called Johnny which meant "friend-pet-brother."

"All right," Johnny said, "but I don't understand."

"You mustn't harm them, either," Baba said. "Remember, I brought you here. Otherwise you wouldn't know where the nests were. Even if you just tell the grownups and they kill them. It would be wrong. I would have—"

Baba was interrupted by a high whistling, shrieking noise, and the whir of wings. So quick you couldn't have followed his motions, Johnny squatted down, curled his feet under him, thrust his hands and forearms into special armor pockets. Six strangely shaped creatures were diving straight at him.

Arrow-birds! A dirty greenish yellow, they were long and slender, over a foot long. One could not tell where their heads left off and their necks began. They were shaped like long arrow points. Their gossamer-thin wings were a blur of motion.

Johnny braced himself so that if they hit him he would not be knocked over. In a fraction of a second they dived within fifty feet of him.

"Go away friend-pets," Baba clicked, as loudly and as fast as he could. "Go away! Bother us not!" He repeated his cry in a kind of chant, so rapidly it was almost a trill.

The shrieking whistle changed to a low hum. The arrow-birds pulled out of their dive. They floated in mid-air, their wings awhirl. One had almost reached Johnny and was hovering in the air only a couple of yards away. It bent its neck out of arrow position and looked straight at him. Its little purple eyes glittered against the yellow green skin of its head.

Then, like a flash, they were gone.

"Whew!" Johnny breathed. He took his hands out of his armor and stood up. He turned around just in time to see the flight of arrow-birds crawl into the holes in the rocks that were their nests. This was Johnny's third secret.

The arrow-birds obeyed Baba!

Right after Baba's voice had changed and his jewel claws had come in, the two had made this astonishing discovery. They had stumbled upon this nesting place, and the arrow-birds, frightened for their nests, had slashed down at Johnny for the first time in his life. But Baba had cried out desperately in his new deep clicks for them to go away. And they had. It was like magic.

Staring up at the sheer cliff, Johnny was excited, but afraid. Such a climb was too dangerous to do just for the fun of it, but Johnny thought he might have a way of saving Baba. Even when they were much younger the little bear had been willing to leave Johnny in order to climb for diamond-wood nuts fresh from the tree. It was the ideal place for Baba to hide. If Johnny could climb up with him they would be able to visit often and Baba was so fond of fresh nuts he might be willing to use it for a hideout.

Johnny hadn't told Baba about his plan. If they could make it to the top he would tell the bear then.

The high shrieking whistle began again.

Johnny suddenly had an idea.

"Friend-pets, friend-pets, bother me not. Bother me not," Johnny clicked quickly, shaping deep clicks just like Baba's in the back of his throat.

As the birds half -pulled out of their dive, the little bear started to speak.

"No, let me keep trying," Johnny clicked. "Friend-pets, friend-pets, bother me not."

At this, the birds hovered about him making squeaking noises, their heads still in striking position.

"They're puzzled," Baba clicked. "They sense something's wrong. They expect to be shot at by people. I'll tell them to go and it will be all right. In a second they could kill you."

"I've still got my armor," said Johnny. "Maybe if I tell them to come here they'll trust me." Johnny spoke the last in English and the words sent the birds fluttering farther away. They seemed to be on the point of making another dive.

Johnny was pale under his helmet, but clicked, "Friend-pets, come to your friend."

The arrow-birds slowly quieted, squeaking among themselves. Their wings humming, they hovered closer and closer. There were five of them. Finally their heads snapped out of arrow position. One of them hovered in very close.

"Come to me, friend-pet," Johnny clicked to it, and held out his hand.

The creature, watching him carefully with its little purple eyes, floated even nearer, its wings humming. Very gingerly it came to a perch on his hand. Its claws were cold and it smelled faintly of meat fruit.

Johnny breathed deep. He was the only human being who had ever made friends with an arrow-bird.

Slowly, while the other birds hovered in the air about him, Johnny drew in his hand and stroked the bird on its folded wings. It shivered under his touch. But, as he did it no harm, the other birds came closer and lit on his arms and his shoulders. One peered into his face. Another poked the air slits of Johnny's helmet with its sharp bill.

"Baba! Baba!" Johnny cried out. "Do you see this? Do you think I could sneak one home with us?"

"Your people would kill him, Johnny," Baba clicked. "Go away, friend-pet," he clicked to the arrow-bird.

The bird looked at Johnny.

"Go, friend-pets," Johnny clicked regretfully to the five birds about him. With a flash of wings they were gone.

"Gosh," said Johnny. "Gosh!" He unzipped and wriggled out of his armor. "Baba, I don't have to wear armor ever any more. Do you understand? I can just walk around like you do!" The words fairly bubbled out of him. Baba was quiet for a moment, frowning.

"Johnny," he clicked, "I've done something wrong. Something very bad. I'm not sure why, but I just know it's wrong. Those are my friend-pets, not yours. If you use the word 'friend-pet' to them, that means you can never hurt them. You must always help them. But they will always try to kill your mother and father. It is all mixed up."

"Gee, Baba," Johnny was frowning now, too. "Come on, let's try the climb and don't worry about it." From one of the armor straps he unhooked a flashlight he always brought along for exploring caves. He fastened it to his belt.

A few moments later the two friends were looking up at the bare rock face that extended three hundred feet straight up.

"Golly, Baba, do you really think you can take us up there?" Johnny asked.

"If you can hold on, I can take you," Baba said from Johnny's shoulder.

"Start up!" Johnny yelled. Baba leaped up onto the wall of rock, his claws cutting into it. Johnny grasped the harness and hooked his toes into a crack in the stone.

V. A Mystery Indeed!

By the time Baba and Johnny had gone fifty feet up the cliff, Johnny felt as if his arms were about to be pulled from his shoulders. The boy helped push with his feet, but that took only a little weight from his arms. Below him there was nothing but boulders and sharp jagged rocks. In spite of that danger, he felt that he could hardly keep hold of the harness. Sweat poured down into his eyes.

"Hurry, Baba," he said through clenched teeth.

"Ledge soon," the little bear clicked. As he speeded up his climb he slapped his claws deep into the rock, making sharp clapping noises that echoed among the boulders below. He stopped short and Johnny saw a place where the rock jutted out a few inches. Gratefully he felt something solid beneath his feet. He couldn't put his whole foot down, but he could rest his arms a little.

"Whew," Johnny said, "doesn't the ledge get wider?"

"In a minute," Baba answered. Crabwise, with Johnny still hanging on, Baba worked along the ledge, which slowly widened until Johnny could stand alone. They were now on the jungle side of the rock.

A few feet farther on, there was a narrow slit in the rock face that widened into a small cave. Deep in the cave's darkness Johnny heard the squeaking of young arrow-birds. As he crept inside he whipped his flashlight from his belt. Purple eyes glittered at him in the circle of its light. There was a flutter of wings. Johnny and Baba started to click at the same time. The fluttering stopped and the birds' heads disappeared into their nests. The cave ended in a pile of large stones. Johnny sat down.

"Boy, do my arms ache!" Johnny said. "How about you, Baba?"

"I can climb," Baba answered. "But can you hold on? We still have far to go."

"Aren't there any more ledges?" Johnny asked.

"Small ones," Baba answered. "None are wide like this one. Do you still want to go up?"

"Maybe we could tie me on some way," Johnny said. "Mountain climbers do it that way."

In a moment the boy and the bear were trying to see what they could work out. Finally Johnny had Baba use the razor sharp point of one of his claws to cut a pair of long thin straps from the wide ones on the harness. These they tied to Johnny's belt and then to Baba's harness again.

When the straps were finished, Johnny felt rested and they started out of the cave. They were stopped by the sight below them.

At the foot of the rock there was a wide space of cleared ground, and then the jungle stretched out. About a half mile away some large greyish beasts were breaking out of the undergrowth.

"Rhinosaurs!" Johnny shouted, pointing. "Golly, a whole herd of them!" There were more than thirty of the huge grey-blue saurians. Even at that distance they could hear the low thunder of the gigantic hooves. The beasts stayed close to the brush, knocking down small trees as they came. Johnny knew that heavy blasters were trained on the rhinosaurs from the guard towers. The guards in the gate towers would have a full view of them. Johnny also knew that unless the beasts began to charge the walls, the guards would not fire. If they did, the whole herd might charge. Topped as they were with electric wires, the heavy fifty-foot high walls would be hard to breach. But rhinosaurs had smashed those walls once. Since then the colonists had thickened and electrified them.

"Remember when they attacked and killed a lot of colonists?"

"I remember," Baba clicked. "Your people killed them, too. That is when your dad made my harness."

Johnny nodded. Because it was made of the skin of an animal the colonists had killed, he had had a hard time getting Baba to wear that harness.

"Let's go!" Johnny said.

This time the going was not so hard for Johnny, though they climbed much farther before he and Baba could rest. The next ledge they reached was not large enough to let them sit. Baba had to hang to the rock, but it didn't seem to tire him.

Three more rests, and slowly but surely they were reaching the top. At the last rest Baba clicked to Johnny in warning.

"The rock is getting softer. If my claws tear away from the rock, just relax and fall with me. I'll grab again further down."

"All right," he said.

Johnny didn't dare look down. He had been climbing with Baba since he was three, but never this high before.

They had gone up only a few more feet when Baba's claws began to slip. Johnny let himself go limp just in case anything happened. Very slowly Baba's claws slipped down the rock. Then they caught hold again.

"We will have to move to the side," Baba clicked.

Johnny didn't answer. It was up to Baba. The little bear scuttled crabwise along the side until he found rock that didn't scale off. Then up they went again. Finally there was a ledge. The two scrambled onto it. Above the ledge was a gap in the rock and some boulders. Then they were on the top!

A faint wind was blowing, and Johnny could hear it sing through the top of the stunted diamond-wood tree growing on the summit.

The top of New Plymouth Rock was flat, a hundred feet or more wide, but with many jutting boulders. Here and there grew small bushes and patches of grass. The diamond-wood tree sprang directly from the bare rock.

With shaking fingers Johnny untied the straps and threw himself down on a patch of green. As he laid there, his breath rustling the grass, he heard Baba pattering about and wondered how the little bear had so much energy left.

"Johnny," Baba clicked, "do you want some berries?" Johnny looked up to see the little bear holding some clear, almost transparent red berries in his paw. The colonists called them antelope berries because they grew mainly in antelope country. At that moment Johnny realized he was very thirsty.

"Thanks, Baba!" He crushed the berries with his teeth and felt the sour-sweet juice trickle down his throat. He suddenly felt thrilled with triumph. He was now where no other human had ever been before!

Johnny was just raising his head to look around when he heard the patter of tiny hooves behind him.

"Look, Johnny!" Baba clicked.

Johnny turned. Running toward them was a herd of the tiniest antelope he had ever seen. They were barely six inches high, their curled horns almost as tiny as needles. Head down, they charged directly at him. Johnny jumped to his feet.

"Friend-pets," Baba clicked gently, "bother us not."

The tiny creatures wheeled about and started back in the direction from which they had come.

"Oh, Baba, don't send them away," Johnny said. Then, remembering his success with the arrow-birds, he himself clicked in a low tone, "Come here, friend-pets. Come here."

The antelope with the longest curled blue horns stopped, turned slowly around and pawed the ground, his long neck arched. It was just seven inches high. Johnny laughed. The regular antelope were seven feet high, but otherwise looked exactly the same as these.

Johnny squatted down and, as he moved, the herd turned and ran, making little whinnying noises. Then they wheeled and returned. The leader pranced closer and closer and came to a halt within a foot of Johnny. It was soft blue all over, marked with spots of deeper purple. Its tiny hooves were blue black, and its eyes glistened with deep purple highlights. Johnny reached out both his hands and laid them before the little creature.

"Come," Johnny clicked. Trembling, the little antelope pawed the grass. Then with mincing steps he came forward and placed his forefeet on one hand, his hind feet on the other. Very slowly Johnny raised him from the ground. The small hooves were sharp and dug into the palms of his hands. The little animal's eyes widened and it snorted in fear. Johnny, afraid it might fall, set his hands back on the ground.

"Go, friend-pet," he clicked. With a bound the creature returned to his herd. Together the antelope leaped high over a small boulder and were gone behind a clump of bushes.

Johnny looked up to see Baba watching him steadily. The little bear looked at Johnny the same way as when he had spoken to the arrow-birds.

"Friend-pet-brother Johnny," Baba clicked, "I am sure I am doing wrong. First the arrow-birds and now the antelopes are your friends. But they are your people's enemies."

"Not the antelopes!" Johnny said. "They fight us some, but we don't ever bother them except for meat."

"Your people kill them," Baba said, as if that settled matters. "Now you can't. You've said they were your friends."

"Is that some kind of rule?" Johnny asked.

"You said they were your friends," Baba repeated. "You help your friends and your friends help you. That is the law and will be the law as the trees stand. Between friend and friend there is no parting more than the fingers of a hand." Baba said this in a sort of sing-song of clicks, like the song of a bird. It was something like a poem.

"Baba," Johnny asked, "how do you know all this? You've never talked this way before." Johnny squatted down before the little bear, whose face was screwed up into a puzzled frown.

"I guess I've always known it," Baba clicked. "But it just came back to me. I don't remember much before I came to live with you, Johnny. But I do remember being in a high tree. There was one like me whom I loved very much, and she sang the song I just sang to you. I remember going to sleep while she sang it. It is a true song, too."

"Would you sing it again?" Johnny asked.

The little bear began again:

"You help your friends and your friends help you. It is the law and will be the law as the trees stand. Between friend and friend there is no parting more than the fingers of a hand."

This time the little bear really sang, trilling the clicks to a tune like the roll of a mockingbird's song. Johnny felt very strange. He patted Baba on the head and then stood up.

"I think I understand," he said, and looked out over the surrounding countryside, thinking about the little antelope he had just held in his hands.

"I'm hungry," the little bear clicked. With a jump and a bounce he started for the stunted diamond-wood tree.

"Baba," Johnny called. The little bear bounced back. "Aren't there plenty of those nuts here for you to live on? I mean, enough to feed you regularly if you lived here all the time?"

The little bear nodded yes, but frowned.

"I want to live with you, Johnny," he clicked.

"I know, Baba. But you're in danger. I hoped that if I could show you I'd be able to visit you, maybe you'd stay."

At the unhappiness on the little bear's face, Johnny hurried on. "Look, Baba, I can't make you stay here. But somebody's going to find out about your nails if you stay with me. If you live here, I could come up and visit you when the nights come, and if we were lucky, I could see you most every wake-time down by the rocks..." Johnny's voice trailed off. Baba was looking unhappier and unhappier.

"I want to live with you," Baba repeated. "Remember what the song says about parting. You stay here with me."

It was Johnny's turn to look unhappy. He didn't want to leave his father and mother, any more than Baba wanted to leave him. The hard climb was all for nothing.

"I can't, Baba. You know that," he said sadly.

"I can't either," Baba said.

Johnny continued arguing for a long time but it did no good. Baba wanted to be with Johnny: there wasn't anything more to say.

"I'm still hungry!" clicked the little bear, plaintively. Then, with a bounce, Baba was up and away. The little bear was crazier about fresh diamond-wood nuts than anything else, even chocolate.

Johnny felt sad and confused. He got up. Below him stretched the sweet green lands of Venus. The hard angles of the walls and the squat grey buildings of the settlements were somehow out of keeping with the rest of the land.

There was an almost park-like look about the jungle from this height. In the distance the towering groves of diamond-wood trees, where the marva lived, shone blue green against the light green clouds that were the skies of Venus. Between the blue groves of diamond-wood were the meadow lands, soft and rolling. At the edges of the meadows were the lower and darker green meat trees, where the saber-tooth leopards stalked. The land was laced with rivers that shone in the green light.

It was all so beautiful, and so deadly. In a few hours evening would begin, bringing almost three Earth days of twilight. Venus turned so slowly that there was a whole Earth week each of daylight and night. But of course people had to sleep and work by Earth days. The thick permanent clouds surrounding Venus glowed with light hours after sundown, making the twilight last and last.

Beyond the marshes was the sea. It, too, was filled with savage life including flying crocodiles who made nests of the bones of their prey, great dinosaur-like monsters and shark-snakes. But none of these dared come onto the land, for the land animals fought them as fiercely as they fought man.

Except for Baba, all the animals on Venus were determined to kill Johnny's people. And he had just been making friends with some of those enemies. He felt strange, as if he were being a traitor to his own kind.

Johnny didn't like that feeling. Suddenly he thought of Baba living among people and wondered if the little bear felt the same way.

Johnny turned away from the edge of the cliff and kicked a stone. He began to wander over the top of New Plymouth Rock, peering into bushes and piles of boulders. He passed near the antelopes grazing on some grass. They lifted their heads and whinnied, but went on grazing. Johnny liked that. Beside a pile of small boulders, he found some arrow-bird nests. He spoke to the birds and all was well.

"That's an odd pile of boulders," Johnny muttered to himself. It didn't look just right, somehow. He pushed one of the stones and it rolled down almost to his foot. There was a dark empty space beyond it. He took his flashlight from his belt and shined it down into the opening.

He almost dropped the flashlight.

The light revealed the shape of a bouncing bear, a marva, just like Baba!

"Baba!" Johnny turned and yelled, "Come here, quick!"

When he looked back, the bear in the opening had not moved. It was not blue, but the color of the rock. Johnny stopped shaking. The opening was the entrance into a cave, and on the wall of the cave was carved the figure of a bear he had thought was alive.

But he was sure that the bear had been blue!

VI. Inside New Plymouth Rock

Johnny and Baba excitedly started clearing away the pile of boulders and stones from the mouth of the mysterious cave. Immediately the arrow-birds began flying around, their heads snapping into striking position.

"They don't like us doing this," Baba clicked. "They don't like it at all." He turned to the fluttering birds. "Bother us not! Bother us not!" he repeated. The birds retreated, but hovered in the air not far off.

"Go away!" Johnny clicked. The birds squeaked among themselves and went a little farther away. "I don't understand," Johnny said. "We aren't bothering their nests." He and Baba each picked up a stone and carried it away from the cave opening. Johnny watched the arrow-birds from the corners of his eyes. They dived in closer.

"Go away," came a firm, deep click. The birds stopped in mid-air and then were gone.

"Gosh," Johnny said to Baba, "you sure made them go that time."

Baba's eyes opened wide.

"I didn't say anything," he clicked.

The bear and the boy looked at one another, puzzled, and then into the opening. The bear cut in the stone was all they could see.

"Come on, Baba!" Johnny rushed to the opening and knocked down a few more stones. Baba pushed them farther away. In a few minutes of hard work the opening was big enough for Johnny to squeeze through. Around the edge of the cave, the rock was carved with the shapes of many animals. The floor slanted sharply downward.

"Hurry, Johnny," Baba clicked anxiously. "He may have gone away." The little bear's eyes were shining with eagerness.

Johnny's heart sank. Baba had not seen another live jewel bear since he had been captured. He had never seemed interested. But now he was quivering with excitement. If they found marva, maybe Baba would want to stay with them! Johnny wanted Baba to be safe, but he didn't want to lose him for always.

The little bear was already scurrying down the steep slope. Without stopping to think of danger ahead, Johnny plunged after him. The ceiling was just high enough for him to stand upright. Flashing his light into the darkness, Johnny saw that the cave was a long passageway that curved down into the heart of the great rock.

Soon they were too deep inside for any light to reach them from the mouth of the cave. Except for the beam of Johnny's flashlight, they were surrounded by complete darkness. The air was musty and cool and their footfalls echoed, making scary hollow noises.

"Stop!" Johnny said. He held his fingers to his lips. His words echoed and re-echoed in front of them. Then there was almost silence. A soft padding and clicking sound came from far in the distance. It was the same kind of noise Baba's feet and claws made on stone.

The two started out again at a half run. The slope was almost too steep, and Johnny had to slide to a halt to keep from falling. Baba went bouncing along ahead and out of sight. As the slope became steeper yet, Johnny had to slide forward carefully. He stumbled and went down on his back. His flashlight slipped from his hand and went rolling on down the passage and out of sight.

In a second it was pitch black.

"Baba," Johnny yelled at the top of his lungs. His only answer was his own voice echoing down the long corridor. He pushed himself up into a sitting position and slid on forward on the seat of his pants, his heart beating rapidly.

A few very long minutes later, he saw a light shining in the distance. It was Baba, the flashlight in his paw.

"Hurry, Johnny!" he clicked. "Hurry!"

With the way lighted for him, Johnny got to his feet and could move faster. As he reached Baba, the passage began to widen and the slope became less steep.

"I saw him," Baba clicked excitedly. "He was big. I'm sure if we could catch him he'd be a friend! I tried to talk to him but he went on ahead just when you called. Oh, Johnny, I do want to find him!"

Johnny had never seen Baba so excited.

Suddenly, the passageway ended and they were in a great underground room. Johnny flashed his light around the walls. They, too, were carved with scenes of life on Venus. Beneath each carving was a small doorway leading into a side room. There was one large doorway opposite the one through which they had entered.

"It looks like a meeting house," Johnny said. "With seats and everything." He flashed the light on one of the carvings. He had heard of carvings like these and had seen one once. His father said that they must have been made by an intelligent life form that had visited Venus from the stars. This cave must have been where they had hidden from the animals, just as men now hid from them behind the settlement's great walls. Johnny was awed.

"Johnny, don't just stand here," Baba clicked. "We've got to find him!"

Johnny looked from opening to opening.

"Which way, Baba?"

The little bear sniffed the air. "I can't tell," he said. "I can't tell." Hurriedly they made a circle about the great room. When they came to the large opening, Baba sniffed carefully.

"Maybe here," he clicked, and plunged through.

Down they went as before. This time Johnny grabbed Baba's harness and they were able to move faster. This corridor was just as steep and curving as the first one.

In a few minutes they emerged into another room. It was smaller than the room above and had three small doorways and one large opening.

"Let's try them all," Baba said. Through each of the three small doorways they entered similar rooms. The fourth opening was another corridor. Again Baba thought he smelled the path of the marva.

Down that corridor they went, down and down. Finally it ended in hundreds large and small rooms; the rock was like a honeycomb. Johnny's flashlight was already growing dim, and they didn't dare try to search much longer.

Trying to follow the scent they took a side corridor that led from one small room to another, and came out into a narrow passageway. A faint light glimmered at the end of it. Baba bounded on ahead, Johnny running to keep up with him.

The light seeped through a pile of rocks. Johnny flashed his light through one of the cracks. Behind the pile of rocks the tunnel continued for several feet. In the light of his flashlight Johnny could see bits of leather on the floor of the outer part of the cave. Just beyond them on the other side of the rocks was the cave Johnny and Baba had rested in while climbing up, the cave in which they had cut the long straps they had used to tie themselves together for the long climb upward. The bits of leather on the floor were scraps that had been left over.

"Why, we're almost to the bottom," Johnny said.

"Yes," Baba clicked. "I guess we can't find him. I don't smell anything now but arrow-birds," he ended sadly.

"We gotta try," Johnny said firmly. He felt hollow inside when he thought Baba might go away for good, but he was convinced now that this was the only way to keep him safe.

"Let's try farther down." Johnny turned around and a few minutes later they were going down one of the curving main corridors again.

This corridor gradually straightened out. Soon it hardly slanted down at all. It finally turned into what seemed to be a long underground tunnel. Johnny had to stoop over to keep from hitting his head on the ceiling.

The passageway was no longer going through solid rock, and its walls and floor consisted of sticky clay. Johnny's and Baba's feet made squishing noises as they walked. It seemed as if the tunnel would never end. They walked on and on.

"I think we're going away from New Plymouth Rock," Baba clicked.

"I think so, too," Johnny answered. "We must've already gone 'most a mile."

The walls had narrowed until Johnny and Baba had to walk single file. Suddenly the passageway slanted upward and a faint glow of light could be seen far away.

As they began to climb toward the light the ceiling became so low Johnny had to crawl on his hands and knees. It was a long, sticky climb.

As they approached within a few yards of the light, Baba stopped, blocking Johnny's way.

"This cave must end up in the jungle outside the colony wall," the little bear clicked. "Maybe we ought to stop." He sounded worried.

But Johnny was not going to let this chance pass.

"Go on," he urged.

"But the rhinosaurs…"

"Who's afraid of an old rhinosaur?" Johnny demanded.

"You are," Baba clicked. But he scrambled on.

They emerged into the blinding light in the center of a tangle of thick, high brush. They were out in the jungle, far away from the rock!

The boy and his bear were covered with mud from head to foot. They peered carefully around, listening. In the distance they could hear the rumble of moving rhinosaurs.

As they crept away from the cave, their view continued to be blocked by large bushes and trees. They couldn't even see New Plymouth Rock. Stepping quietly and carefully they finally came to an opening in the brush. Far to the right was the Rock, and, farther in the distance, a guard tower.

"Get back," Johnny hissed. "The guard will see us." The two jumped back.

There was a grunt behind them. They turned. Behind a screen of brush, a great blue-scaled rhinosaur was waking up. It was between them and the opening to the cave. It snorted with the sound of a deep bass drum, and heaved up on its feet.

Ahead, at the edge of the clearing, was a tall meat tree. They had two chances. They could turn quietly and creep away into the brush, hoping the big beast would not see or hear them. Or, they could make a run for the meat tree in full view of the guard tower.

VII. The Rhinosaur Stampede

The decision was made for them by the rhinosaur. The great scaled beast began to turn around, crashing down brush as he moved. In a few seconds he would be facing directly toward them.

"Tree," Baba clicked very softly. Johnny nodded. The two slinked like hunting cats toward the tree. They didn't dare look back.

"I think the guard saw us," Baba clicked. "He was waving his arms." The jewel bear had already climbed part way up the trunk. He motioned for Johnny to grab the harness.

Not making a sound Johnny took hold of the harness, and the two of them started up the tree. When they reached the first branch, Johnny let go the harness and clambered up as quickly and quietly as he could. Only when they were screened from view by the fleshy leaves of the meat tree did he dare to look down.

Through little openings between the leaves he could see the rhinosaur. It was shaking its ugly horned head. Its little black-blue eyes peered about under blue scaled eyelids. It trumpeted. The deep blasting sound echoed against the settlement walls. For some minutes it moved around in the brush, snorting. It paused, snuffing in air in great gulps. Then it headed straight for the tree and began to trot back and forth under it.

It had smelled Johnny!

Its hoofbeats on the ground made the limb Johnny sat on tremble. If the rhinosaur sensed that Johnny was in the tree it was the end. The tree was easily four feet thick at the base, but a rhinosaur could knock it down with one rush. Johnny and Baba were on the highest and tallest branch, but they were barely twenty feet above its head.

The rhinosaur's shoulder brushed against the lowest branch and the whole tree swayed back and forth as if hit by a hurricane.

Johnny was struck by an idea. "Baba," he whispered, "do you think it might obey you just like the arrow-birds?"

"I don't know, Johnny," Baba clicked softly. "I'll try."

Baba started to climb down. By the slow careful way Baba moved, Johnny knew the little bear was afraid, too. It was an awful chance to take. Johnny was about to call him back, but as he opened his lips, the little bear looked up and grinned.

Down Baba went. He was now halfway down the tree, thirty feet from the ground and level with the eyes of the rhinosaur. It caught sight of him, snorted, and pawed the ground, digging up shovelfuls of dirt with each movement.

"Friend-pet! Friend-pet!" Baba clicked and Johnny suddenly wanted to giggle. Imagine having something that size for a pet!

"Friend-pet!" Baba clicked again, "Go away! Go away! Bother us not!"

The big creature stopped still. Muscles rolled and bunched under the heavy blue-grey scales. Was he going to charge or leave?

They never found out.

There was a roar of motors behind the beast, the clank of metal, the deafening blast of a blaster. The ground shook; leaves showered down on Johnny.

The guards had sent a tank to rescue them!

Things began to happen too fast for Johnny to keep track. The rhinosaur roared with pain and wheeled. It had been hit! It charged toward the oncoming tank. It was one of the colony's light duty tanks, built for speed and quick turns. The driver jockeyed for position. The tank shot down the clearing, turned, and stopped. Its guns were too light to kill the huge beast, so the gunner did not bother to fire again. They were trying to draw the rhinosaur away from the tree.

The rhinosaur's hooves thundered, echoing against the walls and the rocks as it gathered speed. It was almost on top of the tank. With a roar of the motors the tank shot forward. The rhinosaur was going too fast to stop or turn. It plunged on past the tank, bellowing its rage.

Almost immediately the tank screeched to a stop beneath the tree. Its manhole swung open. Rick Saunders' red head emerged.

"Get in here! Quick!" he shouted over the noise of the motor.

Johnny needed no invitation. He was already halfway down the trunk of the tree. Baba jumped from his perch into the open manhole. As soon as Johnny was low enough, he grasped a branch, swung on to the top of the tank, and started down the steel ladder. The tank jumped forward with a lurch.

The rhinosaur was bearing down on them. Their guns roared, but the rhinosaur did not stop. As a hand grabbed him, pulling him inside, Johnny saw the tree topple over as the rhinosaur crashed into it.

"Fire the gate rocket!" someone's shout echoed in the tank. Johnny recognized Captain Thompson's deep voice.

"Check!" Johnny heard Rick answer. Rick was up in the gun turret.

After the outside light, it seemed very dark in the tank. It smelled of grease and the burnt air of cannon fire. There was the swish of a rocket. Johnny knew this rocket was a signal for the guard on duty at the steel gateways to be ready to open up.

The motors were roaring with a high whining sound which meant they were going at full speed. The tank bounced and jolted, shaking Johnny from side to side.

"Get ready for the gate!" warned Captain Thompson from the driver's seat. The tank seemed to be almost flying now. Johnny set himself for a violent turn. Like the doors of the houses, the wall gates were double. Each was a heavy steel portcullis, a great sliding door that could be raised and lowered. When a tank came in the outer gate its weight tripped a switch. That switch turned on motors that made the first gate fall and the second rise.

Otherwise fast moving tanks would have smashed into the second gate.

Johnny slid over to an observation slit. To his left he could see that the heavy steel gate was rising. His heart raced. When being chased by rhinosaurs a driver sped straight along the wall and then turned sharply through the open gate. If he timed it right the rhinosaurs plunged on and the tank was safe. It took split second timing.

They were right by the gate. Johnny grabbed a brace. With a scream of the treads, the tank started into a turn.

"Rhinos on the side!" shouted Rick. His guns blasted.

Captain Thompson fought to straighten the tank out of the turn. Baba was sitting with his paws over his ears, his claws glowing as they came close to light from the observation slit.

There was a bone-shattering crash!

Then Johnny felt himself flying through the air. Everything went topsy-turvy. He banged his shoulder against the side of the tank. Then he felt Baba's furry body against his. Rick's feet seemed to come from nowhere and dig into his back. Johnny grabbed on to something solid and wedged himself in tight.

The tank was rolling over and over. Something crashed against it again and again. There was a heavy thud and the sound of breaking metal. Then everything was still. The motors had stopped. From outside came the roar of guns and the bellowing of rhinosaurs.

Johnny found himself sprawled on top of Rick Saunders. He was terribly shaken. Baba was hanging onto one of the rungs of the steel ladder. It was almost pitch dark. Rick struggled to his feet as Johnny scrambled from on top of him.

"We're upside down," Baba clicked softly to Johnny.

"What happened, Saunders?" Captain Thompson's heavy voice demanded from the driver's compartment. "Didn't Harkness teach you to shoot?"

"Four of them rushed us right at the gate," Rick answered. "Did we make it inside?"

"Think so. Anybody hurt?" Thompson asked.

"Just scratched a little," Johnny answered.

"Good," Captain Thompson grunted. "Is the righting jack O.K.?"

Rick tested a lever.

"O.K."

"Let her rip!"

"Hang on, Johnny," Rick said. "We're going to right her."

Johnny knew just what was going to happen. A tank turned turtle had meant a dead crew until the righting jack had been attached to each of the tanks. Compressed air pushed out two rods fore and aft and flipped the tank right side up.

Johnny braced himself. There was a rush of air. Johnny felt the tank tip slowly under him. Then it went over with a crash. The tank was right side up.

"The gate!" Rick exclaimed.

Just above his head Johnny saw light from the observation slit. He looked out. Then he knew what Rick meant. They and the four rhinosaurs had reached the gate at the same time. The rhinosaurs were inside. They had knocked the tank through the outer gateway and had smashed into the steel door before it was halfway down.

The inner door must have met the same fate for Johnny could see that the sliding steel plates were bent and jammed open. The rhinosaurs had kept after the tank until now it lay fifty yards inside the settlement. Even as Johnny watched, another rhinosaur charged through the opening and headed into the settlement.

Captain Thompson was grinding on the starter and Rick was working up in the gun turret.

"The rhinosaurs got through," Johnny clicked to Baba.

59

"And the tank is broken?" Baba clicked back.

"Yes."

"I have to get out," Baba said. "Maybe I can get the rhinosaurs to leave."

"No, Baba," Johnny said. "They're just plain crazy now."

Captain Thompson climbed down out of the driver's compartment.

"The motor is gone. How are the guns?"

"Out of action," Rick answered. "Must be filled with dirt. We can't do any good here."

"O.K.," Captain Thompson said. "Let's get moving. I'm needed out there!"

Rick undid the wing nuts on the manhole and pushed. Metal squeaked, but the door stayed in place.

"Jammed!" Rick said. "Get me a crow bar out of the box."

Johnny dived for the tool box and came up with a pry bar. He handed it to Rick.

"Hurry, man," Captain Thompson said as Rick went to work. His black angry eyes fixed themselves on Johnny.

"We should have left you out there."

"I'm sorry," Johnny said.

In answer the man cuffed Johnny with the back of his hand. Johnny couldn't be angry. He knew what a rhinosaur raid was like, and this one was his fault.

"Oh, leave the kid alone," Rick said from above.

"Leave him alone!" Thompson snorted, and glared first at Johnny and then at Baba. "The kid and that bear have caused more trouble…"

Captain Thompson stopped talking and stared at Baba. He reached out suddenly and grabbed the little bear by the paw.

"Well, look at this!" he said in a hushed tone.

In the steamy darkness of the tank Baba's nails shone clear and blue. The climbing and running had worn off all the paint.

Thompson held up Baba's paws into the light of an observation slit. He scraped with one of his finger nails.

"Nail polish!" he exclaimed.

The manhole came open with a clang.

"She's open!" Rick called.

Captain Thompson paused only a fraction of a second over Baba and climbed the ladder.

"Lock the kid and bear in the tank," Thompson ordered. "There's less danger here for the boy than there would be in the trip to the wall. You, Rick, go back to the gate. I'll run for headquarters. Make it fast!" Without another word he was up the ladder and gone.

Rick Saunders reached down and patted Johnny on the shoulder.

"Tough luck about your bear, son," he said, and then he, too, was gone. The manhole door clanged and Johnny heard a lock click into place. He hugged Baba to him.

"Gosh, Baba," Johnny said, "what are we going to do now?"

Baba, for once, had nothing to say. Johnny hugged the warm, furry creature closer to him. Tears began to streak down his cheeks. Baba didn't like this. He cocked a blue eye at the boy.

"Don't cry, Johnny!" he clicked. "Come on, stop it!" he pleaded. "Why don't we go up in the turret and see what's happening?"

Johnny wiped his tears away and the two climbed into the gun turret. His stomach tightened. Through the four-inch thick bubble of marvaplast he could see the destruction he and Baba had let loose. The whole settlement lay within view. A half dozen of the giant lizard beasts had turned the colony into a dusty hell. Even within the tank the bellows of the beasts and the roar of guns was almost deafening. Most of the marshberry fields had already been trampled in the mud. One of the concrete houses lay crushed into rubble. Johnny was grateful that almost everyone was at the rocket field.

He gave thanks, too, for Captain Thompson. He could see the big man marshaling tanks into an organized row. They were going to try to herd the great beasts out the open gates.

Johnny turned his eyes toward the gates. Someone had manhandled one of the big blaster cannons into the opening, pointing it into the jungle. His friend, Rick Saunders, ran up to help. A dying rhinosaur lay not far from the muzzle of the gun. Evidently the other rhinosaurs were too sensible or too frightened to try the power of that cannon.

Baba was pulling at Johnny's sleeve.

"Look, Johnny, look!" Baba clicked.

Johnny turned and looked toward the settlement again. A heavy duty hunting tank stood before the settlement stockade and store house. Its heavy cannon spoke once and the door dissolved. Four men leaped from the tank and ran inside.

"They're stealing our claws!" Johnny cried out.

Weighed down by the colony's strong box, the four men came out of the building. Inside that strong box were the colony's precious marva claws!

The four hunters heaved the safe into the tank's carrier and climbed inside. With a spurt of dust, the tank rolled on.

A few minutes later it had fought its way through the rhinosaurs and was passing the place where Johnny and Baba stared out of the turret. As it came up to the gate the hunting tank's manhole opened and a man emerged. He waved to Rick, standing beside the cannon. The red-haired ex-bodyguard waved back. Then he climbed up on the tank and down inside. The tank rolled on out into the jungle.

Johnny stood, shocked and silent. Out that gate went the last valuable thing the colony owned!

"I don't understand," Baba clicked. "I thought Rick was the colony's friend."

"I did, too," Johnny said sadly.

VIII. One Secret is Revealed

It was now early evening and the Venus skies were a deep clear green. It was over an hour since the last rhinosaur had been killed or driven out. The gates had been temporarily repaired. Here and there a small building had been trodden into rubble.

Johnny and Baba were still locked inside the tank which had been dragged away from the dangerous fighting. From the turret they were watching a group of men gathered outside the administration building. Johnny wished someone would come and let them out.

Finally the crowd broke up. One group of men hopped on to the back of a tank and headed toward Johnny and Baba. The rest of the crowd followed on foot.

"I wonder what's up," Johnny said.

Baba shook his head.

"I don't like the looks of it," Johnny went on. "We're in an awful pickle." He looked down at the little bear's paws. He had painted the nails again with the nail polish, but he didn't think it would do any good.

The tank came rumbling to a halt beside them. The two crawled down from the turret. Johnny heard the men working on the lock. The manhole door was opened.

"Come on out, Johnny." It was his father's voice. Baba jumped on his shoulder and Johnny climbed slowly out. Johnny's father and Captain Thompson were standing on top of the tank, surrounded by a crowd of grave-faced Venus pioneers. It was odd. None of the men looked angry. Johnny knew they should be very angry with him. He tried to shape words to say he'd try to make up for the trouble he'd caused, but the words would not come.

Mr. Watson reached out and picked Baba from Johnny's shoulder. He lifted up one of the little bear's paws and looked at it carefully.

"The claws still look black to me," he said. Disappointment, mixed with relief, came over the faces of the men.

"Let me show you." Captain Thompson, not ungently, took Baba from Johnny's father.

The little bear looked straight at Johnny, an odd expression in his deep blue eyes. But he didn't struggle.

Captain Thompson set Baba down on the top of the tank and took one of the paws in his hands. With his fingernail he scraped at one of the claws, then another and another. He held the paw up for the men to see. The claws glowed clear blue in the evening light.

"You see," he said, triumphantly, "it is just as I said. The boy has been covering them up." The crowd sighed with wonder.

Captain Thompson turned back to Johnny's father. "You'd better tell the boy right away. It will be easier."

Many of the crowd nodded their agreement. For the first time Johnny made out the object that Captain Thompson had been carrying. It was a small cage made of diamond-wood.

Johnny's father reached out and touched him on the shoulder.

"You know what happened here today, don't you, Johnny?" he asked in a grave tone.

"Yes, sir," Johnny answered in a low, shamed voice. "The crop's been ruined, and those hunters stole our claws."

"That's right," his father said. "And I think you also understand that if it hadn't been for you, this needn't have happened."

"Yes, sir." The words were almost a whisper. Johnny felt the tears coming up into his eyes.

"You can understand, then, it's up to you and us to make amends to the colony."

"Yes, sir." Johnny's whisper was even lower.

"Well, son, I'm sorry to do this, but I have to. I know Baba has been your pet for a long time, but you are going to have to give him up. I've just given him back to the colony. Now, get him into the cage, so we can get this over with."

"But you'll kill him!" Johnny cried out. He reached down and swept the little bear into his arms.

"No, son, not right away," his father answered. "The rocket captain says the colony could make some money by showing him alive on Earth before they, uh, put him to sleep."

"But you know that he'll die. Oh, Daddy, please don't!" Johnny looked up, pleading, at his father.

Frederick Watson's eyes met Johnny's. They were kind but stern. He shook his head firmly.

Johnny looked around him through his tears. Baba was warm and furry in his arms. The men stood about; their faces were grave and determined. Most still held blasters in their hands. Even at that, Baba had a chance. Johnny began to click in the ear of the little bear.

"Baba," he clicked very softly, "you can get away, over the wall by the rock. It isn't very far. I'll throw you as far as I can. If you bounce like crazy they could never hit you."

But the little bear jumped to the steel tank top.

"No, Johnny," he clicked. "You are my friend-pet-brother, no matter what happens."

Then, just as if he had been told to go by Johnny, the little bear walked over to the cage. Captain Thompson was holding a sliding door open. Baba climbed in. He squatted there and made a little whimpering noise that was the only sound he could make beside his clicks. He waved a paw at Johnny.

"The little devil acts almost human," the old guard, Jeb, said from the crowd.

Only Johnny knew how true that was.

"Better hustle that kid inside a tank," someone shouted. "He hasn't got any armor on."

Frederick Watson's head jerked around. His eyes widened. In one motion he took Johnny into his arms and jumped to the ground. Seconds later Johnny was in a big hunting tank headed for home, a home for the first time in ten years empty of a little bouncing bear.

IX. The Price of a Brother

Johnny had some tall explaining to do about his lack of armor. He was in a tight spot, for the less he let anyone know, the more chance he had to find some way of rescuing Baba.

Johnny was very careful about his explanation. There might still be a way. The fact that he had been seen on top of New Plymouth Rock made his explanation easier. He simply said that he had been looking for a place to hide the little bear and, in order for Baba to help take him up the rock, he had had to risk taking off his armor. He said nothing about Baba and the arrow-birds.

Being found in the jungle was harder to explain without telling a lie, but he managed it. He said that he and Baba had taken a route down that had made them land on the jungle side of the rock. It didn't explain why they were beyond the clearing, but his parents seemed to assume that he had been trying to get among the brush where he could hide from the animals. He said nothing at all about the caves in the rock. It was a pretty thin story, but his family was too relieved that he had come home alive to worry much about it.

It was long past supper time when the explaining was over and his mother began to prepare a meal.

Ordinarily Johnny's father would not have been home even for supper. Rocket Day was a busy time for the leader of the colony. But with all the confusion, the business of the day had to be put aside.

It was a strangely sad and silent house. Johnny himself was so good his parents could hardly recognize him. He had showered without being asked and changed into clean clothes. His hands were perfectly clean at the table. His mother had hidden Baba's high chair away; the little bear had always sat with them at table. It was a quiet meal.

Often after the before-sleep meal Johnny and his father worked on model rockets, but this evening models were forgotten. Johnny got a book and his father busied himself with papers. But Johnny didn't read. He kept thinking of Baba, all alone in the settlement storage house, surrounded by guards. The whole area was lit up in case hunters should try to steal the little bear just as they had stolen the marva claws.

The family sat in silence. Once Johnny saw his mother wipe a tear away from her eyes. He knew she liked Baba, too. But she liked him only as a pet.

"Dad," he said suddenly. His father looked up from his work. "Would you—" Johnny didn't know how to put the question he had to ask. "I mean, well, the colony's in pretty bad shape, isn't it?"

"Yes, son," his father said gravely, "it is."

"The million dollars we get for Baba will help out a lot, won't it?" Johnny was very serious. "But, without it, would everybody starve to death?"

"A million dollars will help the colony out," his father answered. "But even without it, nobody would starve. There are the meat fruit and berries to gather and the animals to hunt. But everyone would have a very hard time. It isn't a simple thing to keep a colony going. It is very difficult and very important. Mankind is reaching out, son, and some day we may inhabit planets of all the stars in the heavens. But only if our Venus colony succeeds. It is a big thing, Johnny." Mr. Watson's voice was serious, as if he were talking to another man. Johnny was quiet a minute.

"Dad," he said slowly, "in order to get that million dollars would you have mother or me," he paused, "put to sleep?"

"Johnny!" Johnny's mother broke in in a horrified voice. "That's no question to ask your father."

"I've got to know, Mother. I've just got to," Johnny said earnestly, his brow wrinkled.

Johnny's father looked at him strangely.

"Did you really think," he asked in a tight, hurt voice, "I would do a thing like that?"

"Not even Uncle Nathan?" Johnny persisted. Nathan was his mother's brother. Johnny wasn't sure why, but he had the impression his father didn't care for Nathan.

"All right, Johnny," his father said in a firm voice. "I'll answer you. No, I wouldn't have you, your mother, or your Uncle Nathan 'put to sleep' for any amount of money. Not for the colony or for myself. But you must understand, Johnny, you aren't the same as a little bouncing bear."

"But Baba—" Johnny began.

"Baba is an animal," Johnny's mother broke in. "I know how you love him. But you have to understand that your father could not do differently from what he did." She came over to Johnny and put her arm around him. "We love Baba, too, and it hurts us to give him up. Still we must. You do understand, don't you?"

Johnny looked up into his mother's face and smiled. It was a very small and very weak smile, but a smile none the less.

"I understand," he said, and turned back to his father. "Thanks for answering my question, Dad." Johnny felt better for the first time since Baba had been put in the cage. Now he knew just what he had to do. It was right to do it. Baba was as close to him as any brother.

"Do you think I could go see Baba before sleep time, Dad? You know he won't eat if I'm not there."

Johnny's father looked at his mother.

"It couldn't do any harm, Fred," she said. "Let the boy go. But he must be in bed soon."

"All right, son," his father answered. "But remember, the whole thing is out of our hands now. You'll just have to accept what is going to happen."

"O.K., Dad," Johnny said. Everything was going to be all right, but he'd need every ounce of courage he had.

A few minutes later Jeb, the old guard, let Johnny and his father into the store house.

The little bear sat quietly in his cage. There were a dozen uncracked nuts on the floor. An untouched bar of chocolate lay beside him.

"I'm sure glad to see you!" said old Jeb. "Ever since he got here the little critter's been sitting just like that, kind of crying to himself. He wouldn't pay attention even when I gave him the chocolate."

"He'll be all right now," Johnny's father said.

"It probably oughtn't to bother me so much." Jeb closed the door and stood there with them. He took off his helmet and scratched his head. "But my partner'n me caught one of the little ones once. We watched it just waste away, crying like that all the time. I always figured we should have let it go. But then there was always the chance it'd grow up and be worth a million." He glanced down at Johnny, who was removing his armor, and came to a stumbling halt. "Sorry, kid," he said. He put his helmet back on and went out.

As soon as he saw Johnny, the little bear's ears perked up.

"Hi!" he clicked.

Johnny winked.

Johnny's father stood there and watched them.

"Remember, Johnny," he cautioned, "this is just a visit. What the colony decides in this matter goes."

"I know, Dad," Johnny answered.

"I'll be back in half an hour," his father said. "Get him to eat, if you can. Night will be here in a few hours and he'll sleep then." With this he opened the door and left.

Johnny rushed to the cage. His hand was on the latch when the door opened again. It was old Jeb.

"Sorry, son, but I got orders not to leave you alone with the critter. If he ever got out he'd be mighty hard to catch." Jeb walked over and seated himself on a box.

"That's all right," Johnny said, and squatted down in front of the cage. It wasn't part of the plan for Baba to get away – yet. "Besides, he wouldn't run away while I'm here," he said.

"Can't take no chances." Jeb sprawled out as if glad to be off his feet. Johnny turned to Baba.

"Baba," Johnny clicked in the marva language, "can you get out of here, if you want to?" Johnny didn't like to talk in the clicking language with Jeb around, but there was no avoiding it.

"Yes," the little bear answered after a time. But then he whimpered again.

"Doggone it, stop that!" Johnny said in English. Then he clicked, "If things work out right, you aren't going to have to go to Earth or get killed."

"But how?" Baba asked. He seemed to revive a little. "If I got out and came to you they'd just bring me back here."

"I know, but they don't think you're smart enough to do anything else. They don't know anything except that we were up on the rock."

The little bear grinned. Then suddenly he began to sniff. He looked all around him, found the chocolate and began to stuff it into his mouth, making loud smacking noises. Johnny gave a sigh of relief. Baba was on the mend.

"Now, listen, we've gotta make plans."

"But what can we do, if they know we were on the rock?" Baba clicked through a mouthful of chocolate mixed with nut. It was his favorite combination.

Johnny took a deep breath. "We could run away into the jungle!" he clicked. He jumped when Jeb moved away from his box.

"That's quite a racket you two are making." Jeb walked over and peered at them from under jutting grey eyebrows. "Well, you've got the little devil to eating'!" He smiled and waved at Baba. Baba waved back and the guard laughed. "It's a pity, that what it is. It's just a pity you're worth so much money!" He went back to his seat.

"But, Johnny," Baba clicked, "you couldn't live in the jungle."

"You can't live here or on Earth. Sooner or later they're going to – well, they're going to want your claws and teeth. Out there we would have a chance. Why, we might even find some of the –." He put in the word 'wild' in English, for there was no word for it in the clicking language. "– marvas, and we could live with them."

"No!" Baba interrupted. "You might be killed. I can make the arrow-birds go away; but there are the horned snakes, and the leopards, and rhinosaurs, and –."

"Wasn't that old rhinosaur about to go away?" Johnny broke in. "Just because you said so?"

"Maybe," Baba admitted. "He stopped a second. But then we don't know for sure!"

"I've got to take the chance. I've just got to!" Johnny insisted. "I can't let them take you away and use you for making somebody's rings or a mess of plastic. Remember that song you sang?" Johnny tried to sing the little lullaby that Baba had sung on the top of New Plymouth Rock. The little bear grinned and put his paws over his ears.

"The words are right," he said, "but the tune is all wrong. Listen!" The little bear sang the song that was like the roll of a mockingbird's call.

"That's right pretty," Jeb said from his box. "I'd heard men say that the critters sang, but never did hear one myself. Old hunter friend of mine said he came on a marva once singing to her little ones that way. It was so pretty he stopped to listen and by gum if she didn't smell him and bounce off before he could draw a bead on her."

"Baba sings real well when he's happy," Johnny said, and turned back to Baba. "And you sing true, too, Baba," he clicked.

"All right," the little bear clicked. "How will we do it?"

The plan came out in a rush. Johnny had it all worked out. "It's Venus evening now," Johnny said, "and we're supposed to be in a sleep period. That means there won't be too many people up but guards. I'll take some food for me and some matches and a flashlight and some other things." He paused. "They leave you alone in here, don't they?"

"Yes," clicked Baba.

"Do you think you can cut a hole in the bottom of the cage?" Johnny asked.

"Easy!" The little bear touched a bar with his claws.

"Good. When you're out, dig a hole in the floor. But be careful. They have guards walking all around, and they already have lights rigged up. The switch is in between the double doors. Get your escape holes all made, turn out the lights, and then scoot! I'll be waiting for you by the rock. O.K.?"

The little bear nodded. "We'll have to find a place to be when it gets dark," he clicked. Baba didn't sleep as people did, but during the four day period of darkness he had to sleep most of the time.

"We'll find some place," Johnny clicked. "Now, listen. I'll try to get some sleep and I'll be ready in five hours. Don't try to get out before then. My folks will be asleep and I can slip out of the house. If it takes you longer, I'll wait."

"Leave it to me," Baba said.

They had everything settled and were playing together through the bars of the cage when Johnny's father came after him.

"Time for bed, son," his father said. "Say goodbye, now."

Johnny got into his armor, said goodnight to Jeb and followed his father outside. In the deep green twilight every building of the settlement stood out sharp and clear. A cool breeze was coming up. Johnny looked over to New Plymouth Rock. Behind that towering rock lay the vast and menacing jungle.

X. Alone in the Jungle

Johnny was afraid. Behind a boulder by New Plymouth Rock, he had been sitting and waiting for Baba for almost one hour. It was too long a time to wait with nothing to do but imagine what might happen in the jungle. Johnny was dressed for the cold night to come in a synthetic fur parka. Strapped on his back was a pack containing food and jungle equipment. Beside him was Baba's harness. He was very tired and sleepy.

He leaned over and peeked cautiously from behind the boulder. The lights around the storage shed were still on. He wondered what was keeping Baba. He made himself comfortable again and listened to the night sounds. He listened hard for any sound of rhinosaurs outside. There was only the sigh of wind through the trampled marshberries.

As he listened, his head nodded down on his breast, and his eyes closed. He wished Baba would come. Maybe he couldn't make it. Maybe he... But his thought trailed off into a dream. He was up in the meat tree being attacked by a rhinosaur standing twice as high as the tree. Far away someone began shooting at the rhinosaur. Then the tree was being shaken back and forth. Baba was clicking something in the dream Johnny couldn't understand.

"Wake up, Johnny! Wake up!"

Johnny's head jerked up. The shaking was real. It was Baba pushing his shoulder. The shooting was real too. Men were running about the settlement with flashlights. It was hard to see for any distance through the green twilight which would last for many hours longer.

"Hurry, Johnny!" Baba clicked.

"O.K." Johnny said. He was still dazed with sleep as he helped Baba struggle into his harness. As soon as the harness was on, they began to run deeper among the boulders. Hundreds of small stones under their feet made a sound like a landslide. They stopped still, listening.

The men had not heard.

"Maybe we'd better go straight up the main rock," Johnny said.

Baba nodded. Both knew it would be harder work, but safer. Johnny tested the straps on Baba's harness. There was no time to tie himself on. This time it was going to be harder for both of them.

Baba didn't dare bounce, so they started right from the foot of the rock. In the half-light it was not likely that the men would see them. Even if they did, there was a good chance they would hold their fire when they saw Johnny. If so, the two of them could still get away. Oddly, Johnny's fear was gone.

From below them came the sound of a man moving among the rocks.

"Quiet, Baba," Johnny whispered.

Baba stopped.

Jeb flashed his light among the rocks and up along the main rock. For a fraction of a second the light was full on them. But it passed by without pausing.

"Nothing over here!" Jeb called out in a loud voice. "Dang critter must have got clear away."

There was the sound of footsteps hurrying toward them. Johnny and Baba froze to the rock.

"Hey, you two," Jeb's voice came softly, "I don't know what you're aimin' to do, but you'd better hurry up about it. They're fixin' to mount searchlights on the wall."

Johnny was flabbergasted. The old hunter was helping them!

There was a chuckle from below.

"Hurry up, now. I don't want no more baby marva a haunting me like the one I told you about."

"Thanks," Johnny whispered. "Golly, thanks! Come on, Baba," he clicked, turning his head back to the little bear.

Baba began to scurry along up the rocks once more.

"Just one thing more," the whisper followed them. "Ain't that clickin' the way those critters got of talking?"

"Yes," Johnny answered.

"I figgered it, by gosh!" Jeb chuckled deep in his throat. "I just knew you was fixin' up a getaway. Good luck, you two!"

"Goodbye," Johnny said.

"You are a good man," Baba clicked. "A true friend!"

"Baba said you are a good man and a true friend," Johnny whispered.

"Thank you, Baba," the old man said. Then he was gone.

Baba and Johnny began climbing in earnest now. Johnny couldn't let himself get tired. As silently as they could, they went on and on.

They climbed for what seemed an hour. Actually it was fifteen minutes later when they reached the ledge leading to the cave in the rock. They were barely inside when search lights cut through the twilight and began to play on the rock.

The two sat down to rest, but not for long. Soon they were tearing down the pile of rocks at the back of the cave so they could get into the main caverns. They had talked about staying the night within the inner rooms, but decided it was too dangerous. Sooner or later the colonists were bound to drop someone from a helicopter to search for Baba on top of the rock; and there was too great a chance the entrance would be discovered.

Once inside the main caverns, the first job was to make their way through the long passageways to the top of the rock to block the entrance they had made earlier in the day. It took precious time, but they had to do it. They almost didn't make it, for as they were filling in the last stone at the cave mouth they heard the sound of 'copter motors. Johnny grabbed Baba's harness, and down the long winding passageways they went, full tilt.

Soon they were picking their way about the brush near the exit of the long, damp tunnel. Through the green twilight they could see the searchlights brightening New

Plymouth Rock. Baba was sniffing the air. Johnny listened carefully for the sound of rhinosaurs or of tanks. There was no evidence of either man or animal.

"We made it, Grandfather Bear!" Johnny said aloud to Baba. "You're safe!"

Baba grinned. "No rhinosaurs around either," he clicked. "We'd better hurry."

"Let's stick close to trees for a while; just in case," Johnny suggested. Only heavy brush surrounded them.

"We'd better get to a tank path," Baba clicked, "or we won't get very far very fast."

Johnny nodded. He settled his pack on his shoulder and the two moved forward. Using Johnny's compass they cut through the brush and soon came to a tank path. It was very still. There was no sound but the wind rustling the trees. All around them were trees and brush and pools of deep green shadow.

The first two miles were the easiest. In the absence of rhinosaurs, there was nothing much to fear here but arrow-birds, and they would soon be heading for their nests. Most of the Venus animals kept well away from the settlement. Twice a flight of arrow-birds came shrieking down at them, and twice Baba's clicks sent them whirring on their way. Otherwise the jungle was empty of life. It was a relatively safe zone. But in order to make sure of Baba's safety, they would have to go on into an area of teeming life.

Johnny thought of the comfort and safety of the settlement, of the love and protection his parents had given him. He had left a note for his parents. "I am sorry to take Baba away since he is worth so much to the colony," he had written. "But he is just like a brother to me. Don't worry. I will be safe with Baba." He hoped they would understand.

Though he had bravely told his parents not to worry, here in the jungle, Johnny, himself, was already frightened and very homesick.

"Baba," he said suddenly, "it's going to be hard being away from Mom and Pop." They were walking now through the thick grove of meat trees that edged a forest of diamond-woods that loomed up in the distance.

"Yes," Baba clicked, "I know."

"Well, I was thinking," Johnny continued, "that after we find your people, maybe after a month or so, I could go back home. Later I could come for visits and things." Johnny watched Baba from the corners of his eyes to see how the little bear would take to the idea. For a while, Baba bounded along beside Johnny, his eyes straight ahead.

"I know what it's like being without a mother and father," the little bear clicked so softly Johnny could hardly hear him. "It happened long ago, but I remember how it was at first. I can't bear to think of your going away. But we will see what happens." Baba turned toward Johnny. "I think you shouldn't have come."

Johnny was sorry for having brought up the subject.

"Let's skip it," he said. "Don't be an unhappy old grandfather bear," he joked. "Think about the nuts you'll find right ahead."

The nuts were not really very close. It took a good deal of hiking before the tank trail began to wind among gigantic trees. Bigger than Earth redwoods, they rose almost like mountains around them. Here even the wind did not enter, and beneath their feet was a cushion of fine leaves. All was silence. Johnny was glad to rest his feet while Baba gathered a few nuts. Then they trudged on.

Hours later they emerged from the darkness of the diamond-wood forest into the green twilight of the surrounding meat trees. Johnny was exhausted.

A sudden coughing roar in the distance sent a shiver up Johnny's back and brought them to an abrupt halt. It was a saber-tooth leopard!

Johnny heard a slight stir of movement in the underbrush. About them, birds of all kinds twittered and chirped, readying themselves for the long darkness of Venus night. They were out of the safety zone.

Though many hours had gone by, it was still Venus evening. He and Baba had to push on into the deadly part of the jungle before they could rest.

The leopard's roar had come from far away and there was no immediate danger, but from that time on the two watched every step they took. A faint breeze blew in their faces. That was good. Johnny's scent would not be blown to any of the animals. Johnny set his voice to click, not to speak. He had to try to forget human speech, and talk always like Baba. He spoke to Baba constantly in the marva language, and Baba corrected him when he let his clicks become high pitched as Baba's once had been.

The meat tree grove was thinning out. The tank tracks were getting fainter and fainter. Vines wound around the trees and bushes. On the vines great orange flowers seemed to burn with color in the green light. Johnny watched the flowers carefully because one might really be a scarlet ape. Men called these flowers monkey flowers since they were so near the color of those small apes that lived on the edge of meat tree groves. As the two adventurers walked, the noises of animals became louder and more numerous. A large bird fluttered across their path and went shrieking ahead of them.

Then there was sudden silence. They stopped.

Baba hurriedly clicked loudly into the silence, "Friend-pets, friend-pets, bother—"

He did not have time to finish the sentence. Johnny was struck suddenly on the back and sent sprawling on his face. A hundred tiny hands seemed to be pulling at his hair. He felt a rip of cloth and then a sharp pain as a small claw cut into his back. Baba was clicking loudly.

As suddenly as he was struck down, the attack on him stopped. Dazed, he painfully got to his hands and knees.

"Friend-pets, bother us not. Bother us not!" Baba was repeating over and over again as loudly as he could. Johnny's eyes widened.

Surrounding them were hundreds of tiny monkeys no more than eight inches high. Scarlet red in color, they sat perfectly still, their eyes fixed on Johnny and Baba. Sitting high on a nearby bush one of the little apes held a packet of Johnny's food in its tiny hands. Johnny stood up to his full height and a low growl went up from the animals. The monkey with Johnny's packet hurled it at Johnny with surprising strength. Johnny made a quick catch.

"Thank you," Johnny clicked in the marva tongue. The monkeys chattered excitedly. "Thank you, friend-pet."

"Give it something," Baba clicked. "Oh, I'm afraid, Johnny. They hate you so much! I can feel it." Johnny knew why. The skins of these animals were much in fashion for coats back on Earth.

Johnny reached down for his knife to cut the strings of the packet. As the knife came in sight a menacing growl went up. As Johnny and Baba stood there, more and more of the monkeys leaped from the bushes to join the crowd. The whole path was covered; the trees seemed to be filled with red flowers. Some of the newcomers were intent upon rushing Johnny when the knife glittered in the half-light. But Baba stopped them with his sharp, repeated commands.

Johnny cut the packet open. Among other things, a large bag of candy was inside. He had raided the cupboard well. Johnny then slowly put his knife away.

"Come here," Johnny clicked, as firmly as he could manage. "Friend-pet, come here." He pointed at the little creature who had thrown the package at him. Showing its teeth and growling faintly, the monkey bounded forward. Johnny held out a piece of candy to it. It sidled up, snatched the candy, and ran back to the others. It sniffed at the sweet, chattering wildly. Then its long black tongue went out and licked it. The monkey's eyes widened and it popped the candy into its mouth, smacking its lips.

Again Johnny was almost knocked down. He was surrounded, climbed over, patted, peered at, and deafened by chatter. In a few seconds not a piece was left.

But the monkeys no longer growled.

"Go away! Go away!" Baba clicked. Reluctantly the animals parted from Johnny and took to the trees along the path. The branches swayed under them as they chattered among themselves.

Suddenly, as quickly and mysteriously as they had appeared, the monkeys were gone. Something was wrong! Johnny's fear returned with the sense that something was watching him.

Hardly daring to, he looked behind him. There in the half-darkness, glowed three pairs of green eyes. Crouched ready to spring, a leopardess was watching them, her two cubs beside her. How long they had been watching, Johnny never knew. He froze in his tracks. Baba had not looked around.

"Friend-pets, bother us not, bother us not!" Baba was clicking loudly in preparation for going forward. As Johnny watched, the leopard, followed by her cubs, slipped into the jungle.

"You didn't see her," Johnny clicked. "There was a leopardess and two cubs."

Baba turned in the direction toward which Johnny was pointing. "We'd better go back," he clicked.

"No," Johnny insisted bravely. "She and her cubs went away when you began to talk."

"Not far away." Baba sniffed the air. "I can smell them. I smell rain too."

"Then we'd better find shelter. C'mon. Maybe we better take a path over to the right, away from the tank trail," Johnny suggested. "The leopardess went the other way."

Baba nodded.

They trudged on and took the first animal trail to the right. Baba went slightly ahead, crying "Friend-pets, bother us not!" over and over again. It was almost a chorus now. Most of the time Baba clicked it, but when he got tired Johnny took over for a while. They never ceased repeating the magical words.

Once an antelope walked by their sides a few yards off, but he soon bounded away. Shortly afterward Johnny thought he saw a large black shadow moving in the deep brush.

They walked steadily and found nothing but brush land. Then, not a hundred yards from them, a river shone through the deepening twilight. The shine of the water stopped them. They had proved they could control some of the animals, possibly even the leopards and rhinosaurs. But, if a river snake struck without warning as the monkeys had done, it would be the end of Johnny.

While Johnny stood where he was, Baba went forward, chanting the cry of "Bother us not" as he went. When he returned he looked worried.

"It is too dangerous to try to swim," he clicked. "In some places the branches of the trees on this side almost touch branches of the trees on the other side. If we keep on the path, maybe we can find a place where it would be safe to climb over." The path they were on turned and followed the river.

They walked on for a few minutes. Baba stopped again, sniffing the air.

"I don't like it," he clicked. "The leopards are close again."

They moved forward cautiously, but when minutes passed and no attack came they walked with more confidence. The magic formula of clicks seemed to be working. Though nothing bothered them, they knew from rustling noises and from cries that animals were all about them. Nowhere could they find a place where the tree branches made a bridge across the river. Nowhere could they find a place of refuge.

The trail began to lead away from the river toward a little hill that stood in black outline against the almost darkened sky. Big Venus fireflies had begun to come out, sparkling like so many blue stars. The two weary travelers followed the path, hoping it would lead back to the river. It ended completely at the base of the small rocky hill.

So tired he almost wanted to cry, Johnny sat down in the middle of the path. Then he noticed a spot of deeper darkness among the rocks. He jumped to his feet.

"Hey, Baba," he said, "it looks like a cave! Come on!"

The two of them hurried forward. A nice comfortable cave was just what they were looking for! They were within a few yards of the cave, when they heard a crashing noise from the underbrush and the pad of soft footsteps.

A leopardess leaped in front of them, cutting them off from the cave. The big cat growled low, and two cubs scuttled through the entrance. The leopardess sat back on her haunches in the mouth of the cave, her eyes two gold-green lights burning in the dark green of the late twilight. Slightly larger than an Earth lion, the Venus saber-tooth leopard is coal black, marked with golden spots. Her two tusk-like fangs show why leopards are among the most deadly fighters of all the Venus animals.

Baba began clicking again.

Johnny stood stock still. The leopardess watched them. She looked as if she might spring at any moment. Then, with a ripple of her powerful shoulder muscles, she lay down in the mouth of the cave.

"Let's go before she changes her mind and attacks," Johnny said.

"No, wait!" Baba said. "You stay here."

Slowly Baba walked up to the spot where the big cat was lying, clicking as he went. She appeared to pay no attention to him, but when he was right beside her, she stood up. She made a low rumbling in her throat that sounded strangely like a purr.

When Baba paused, the leopardess made a little coughing sound. The two cubs, who were as large as collie dogs, came tumbling out of the cave, their tongues hanging out. They came up to Baba, cocking their heads. They rubbed themselves in a friendly way against the little bear.

"Come on, Johnny," Baba clicked. "I think we have a home."

His heart in his mouth, Johnny walked forward.

"Friend-pet," he clicked firmly, "I am your friend." Repeating this, he walked straight up to the deadly beast. He reached out a trembling hand and patted the ugly fanged head. The creature stood rigid. But as he petted her, she relaxed and the purring noise began in the back of her throat. The big head moved around. Her mouth opened slightly and she licked his hand. She made a little coughing noise and the cubs came up to him. He petted them, too, and looked at Baba.

"Come on," said the little bear, "let's see what the leopard's house is like."

Together the two explored the inside of the cave with the help of Johnny's flashlight. It was surprisingly clean. The big cat had dragged in straw, which was arranged thickly over part of the floor.

"It sure looks like it would make a good bed," Johnny said. He was so tired; so much had happened. Trader Harkness and the meat fruit, the climbing of New Plymouth Rock, the rhinosaur raid and Rick's betrayal, and the escape into the jungle. Johnny ate a few antelope berries to quench his thirst, but nothing more. He arranged a place for himself on the dried grass and curled up. He was almost asleep, when he heard the big cat come into that part of the cave.

He opened his eyes to see the saber-tooth leopard looming over him. For a second he was afraid. Then, just as a house cat will do, she pushed her paws back and forth into the straw, circled a few times, and lay down right by his head, pushing him aside. He rearranged his bed and lay his head against her soft flank.

With his head pillowed against a saber-tooth leopard, Johnny Watson slipped off to sleep.

XI. The Friends are Separated

Johnny was hot and sweaty. He was glad to see the cool dark cave ahead. It was like home to him by now. The mother leopard was lying in front of the cave, and the two cubs came running to greet them.

"Hi, Pat. Hi, Mike," he called. They came up to be petted.

"They seem happy to see us," Baba clicked as he bounced along.

"And I'm glad to see them," Johnny said. "Golly, I'm hot."

Baba and he had just been down the river trying to find a place where they might cross. Immediately after the long Venus night was over, they had gone exploring in hopes of finding a colony of wild marva nearby. But the only diamond-wood groves close to the cave were still too close to the settlement. The marva must have left them because of the danger. The two had gathered a good supply of nuts for Baba, but otherwise the trip had been useless. Though they were still afraid of the horned river snakes, there was no way of avoiding crossing the river. If they went downstream they would soon be in the rhinosaur marshes. Upstream the river curved back toward the colony.

Johnny and Baba had spent the whole long night in the cave and Johnny had got to know the leopard family quite well. He had discovered they, too, had something like a language. It was made up of different kinds of growls. Each growl meant something, but there weren't many of them. The mother leopard could say things like "Come," or "Go" to her kittens. She had a different growl for each of them, though Johnny named them Pat and Mike. Throughout the time Baba was asleep Johnny had practiced these growls, until he could talk a little in the leopard language. He had also taught the little ones to like meat fruit roasted over the open fire he had had to light to keep warm. All three cats had been afraid of the fire when he had first lit it. They had soon learned it was harmless if they didn't step into it. They were very smart animals, but by no means as smart as Baba. Baba was just as clever as a person.

All the rest of the animals now seemed friendly, too. Johnny thought he knew why. Not only the leopards, but all the animals could talk! They couldn't say much, but just enough to tell one another Johnny wouldn't hurt them. And all of them could understand the marva language. He and Baba talked about this, but they weren't yet ready to take a chance on river snakes. The snakes stayed deep in the water and struck before they could be seen. It didn't seem likely that they would have learned Johnny was a friend.

Baba was going to go down to the river by himself. Perhaps he could find one of the horned snakes and bring it back with him. Then Johnny could make friends with it. If what Johnny thought was true, then the snake would tell the others and he and Baba could float safely across the river on a log they had found.

After patting the mother leopard on the head, Johnny took off his pack and laid it in the mouth of the cave.

"I think I'll go over to the waterfall and have a shower," he said.

"That's not such a good idea," Baba said. "Stay here. I won't be gone long."

"Oh, stop worrying, Grandfather!" Johnny laughed. He was stripping himself down to his shorts. The three leopards sat on their haunches watching him. They were fascinated by his clothes. The first time he had taken them off they had been almost afraid of him.

"I'll take Mama Leopard along with me for a guard," Johnny said. "You tell her, Baba. Maybe I can growl better than you, but she still seems to do everything you say."

Baba clicked directions to the leopard. She was to go along with Johnny and protect him. When Baba was through clicking, the mother leopard came over and licked Johnny, making a growling sound that meant she understood.

Then with a wave of his paw, Baba bounced away toward the river. Johnny was happy to see him go. Baba, himself, had suggested that the trip be taken. It was the first time he had ever offered to leave Johnny for such a long time. Johnny loved the little bear, and it was fun in the jungle, but he couldn't help wishing he were home.

The waterfall was not much of a waterfall. A little way from the leopard's cave was a small spring high up in the rocks. A tiny stream of water fell about ten feet making a great spray and quite a little noise. It made a wonderful shower.

The mother leopard lay on the rocks below while Johnny climbed up to the waterfall. Johnny danced about as the cool water hit his hot dusty skin. It felt wonderful running all over him. Then he walked into a pool and splashed happily.

Then Johnny began to sing. With him the little waterfall sang a tinkling, merry rune that blotted out even the chatter of the birds in the surrounding trees.

It did not blot out a coughing roar that came from the mother leopard. Johnny knew that sound. It meant come!

Johnny stopped singing and looked down. The leopardess was on her feet now, looking into the sky. Johnny looked too. A helicopter floated soundlessly overhead, its jets off.

Johnny looked around for some place to hide. There was none.

The mother leopard crouched. Her muscles rippled under her black and gold skin. In one mighty spring she was beside him. Before Johnny knew what was happening, her great jaws opened – and closed around him. The long saber teeth barely touched his skin.

With no more effort than if she were carrying a feather, she leaped through the air with Johnny in her mouth. When she landed Johnny's feet thumped painfully against a rock. Where she was holding him about the middle in her teeth, he was unharmed.

Johnny heard the roar of gunfire as the helicopter's motors were switched on. Still carrying Johnny in her jaws, the mother leopard screamed in pain. Johnny was tumbled to the ground, half dazed.

A very shaken Johnny watched the mother leopard run away a short distance, then turn and spring back toward him. A second later she was standing over Johnny, putting her body between him and the helicopter. She roared her defiance at the machine. Johnny marveled at her courage. She started to pick him up again.

The helicopter was getting into a position where it could hit the big cat without hitting Johnny. In a few seconds the courageous animal would be dead.

"Run, friend-pet!" he clicked loudly. "Run! They won't hurt me. Run!" She looked down at him and growled in a questioning way. Her muscles tensed, and, with a great spring, she was gone. The guns roared, but the leopard's last bound carried her safely into the brush.

Before Johnny could get to his feet the 'copter was beside him. Two men in armor and helmets jumped out.

"Hurry," yelled the pilot from inside. "You just grazed the leopard."

One man grabbed Johnny by the heels, the other by his shoulders. With one swing he was tossed heavily onto the floor of the 'copter. The two men jumped in after him. The armored door clanged closed. The motors roared and they were going straight up into the sky.

Johnny lay quietly on the floor for some moments; he was still dazed by his fall – and by the sudden turn of events.

"That leopard was crazy," one of the men was saying. "I never saw one come back like that, except for a cub!"

Johnny looked up into the face of the speaker. It was a thin, narrow face with full red lips and small black eyes. Johnny didn't know him.

"That was a narrow squeak you had," the hunter said to Johnny, in a high, nasal voice. "Two minutes later you'd have been leopard food. Are you hurt?"

Johnny sat up slowly, moving his arms and legs.

"Uh uh," he said.

With a whine of the motors the 'copter went into a hover. It floated over the spot where they had picked up Johnny.

"What in the name of all the moon devils were you doing out there like that? Stark naked and no armor?"

"Taking a bath." Johnny was too bewildered to make up an excuse.

The man raised his black eyes to heaven and looked at his companion. "Crazy!" he muttered. "But, kid," he addressed Johnny, "what made—"

"Skip it!" the pilot said, in a low hard voice. The black-eyed man stopped abruptly. Johnny decided the pilot must be the leader. The man turned around and looked at Johnny. He was a large man, slope-shouldered but powerful. His blond hair was slicked down against his head. Two long red scars cut across a white heavy-jawed face. His eyes were so pale they were almost white.

"Where's the bear?" he snapped.

Johnny was struck silent. They were after Baba!

"Come on, kid," the low voice came again, "where's the bear?"

"He ran away." Johnny blurted out the first thing he could think of. "We got lost in the jungle and he ran away, right at first. I lit fires to attract attention and keep off animals, and the rains put them out and my matches got wet. I've had an awful time, and…"

"You ain't seen nothing of the bear?" the scar-faced pilot cut in.

Johnny crossed his fingers carefully and looked the big man straight in the eyes.

"Not since right at first!"

The pale eyes bored into his. Johnny's eyes dropped down.

"The kid's lying!" the big man said to the others, and turned back to Johnny. "O.K., kid, let's have it straight now!"

But no matter how much they questioned him or how they threatened, Johnny insisted he did not know where Baba was.

Finally Ed, the blond scar-faced leader, gave up. He turned to the others. "You guys search the ground," he commanded, "while I call in to the boss." He turned and dialed the radio telephone on the instrument board of the 'copter.

"Hello," he said, "I want to speak to the boss." There was a pause. "Hello," he said again. "We got the kid. Found him where Stevenson thought he saw the fire."

Johnny heard a voice coming back over the instrument. He thought he recognized it, but he couldn't make out any words.

"No," the pilot spoke into the instrument, "the kid says the bear ran away, but I think he's lying. We're going to search from the plane. Can't send anybody down because of the leopards. One had the kid when we found him." There was another pause. "No, not hurt. When we're finished I'll drop him at the colony." There was a long pause. Johnny caught the words, "if I know that bear," and then there was more he couldn't catch.

"That's a smart idea," the scar-faced man said. "We'll do just what you said. O.K. Be seeing you!" The pilot turned back to the other two, who had binoculars trained down into the jungle.

"See anything, Barney?"

"Not a thing, Ed!" the black-eyed man replied.

"You, Shorty?"

The other man shook his head. "Not even a bird."

For over an hour they searched. While they were searching, Ed, the pilot, put in another call and told someone else what had happened. He hinted that even if they didn't find the bear, there was still a way they might get their hands on him.

Johnny sat with his fists clenched. He knew they would shoot if Baba showed himself.

After an hour went by and the 'copter had gone over every foot of the surrounding territory, the men had to give up because they were running low on fuel.

As they went higher up, Johnny peered out. The 'copter veered Venus east – away from the colony. At that moment Johnny's heart sank. The hunters weren't taking him home! Baba would have seen the 'copter

103

come and go. The little bear would think anyone finding Johnny would take him back to the settlement. Johnny knew just what the little bear would do. He would go back to the settlement looking for Johnny!

Johnny had succeeded in keeping those hunters from getting Baba; now the colonists would get him. Or would they? Suddenly Johnny knew whose voice that had been on the radio telephone. The voice was that of the trader. Willard Harkness!

XII. The Price of a Boy

They were in the air over two hours, traveling at maximum speed, before they arrived at their destination. This turned out to be a small cabin, surrounded by the usual high wall, with a space inside the wall for a helicopter and a tank. It was a hunters' hideout entirely hidden from view by diamond-wood trees. The pilot had had to work his way through branches and then fly for a time between the trunks of the great trees before hovering in for a landing. A man was standing in the yard waiting for them when they landed.

As soon as Ed shut off the 'copter's motor, the man who was waiting for them yelled, "No arrow-birds that I can see. Tell the kid to run for it." The man had been informed about him by the helicopter's radio.

"O.K., kid, scoot!" Ed jabbed Johnny in the ribs.

Johnny scooted. The lodge door slammed behind him and he opened the inner door. The large central room was surprisingly neat. The floor was bare but polished. Some hunting trophies were on the windowless walls.

Chained on a perch in one corner of the room, a miserable little scarlet ape sat huddled up, with its chin upon its knees. When it saw Johnny it screamed and chattered. Johnny walked toward it, about to click a greeting.

"Better watch out!" A red head was thrust from the door of another room. "Ed's monkey is meaner than he is." It was Rick Saunders.

"Glad to see you safe!" The big red-haired man grinned easily, and waved.

"Hullo," Johnny said. He didn't smile. If Rick were here, it meant only one thing. These were the same men who had stolen the colony's marva claws! He all but glared at Rick Saunders standing in the inner doorway.

"You don't seem too happy about being rescued," Rick said with a laugh.

"I wasn't rescued. I—" Johnny stopped. He knew he shouldn't have said that.

Rick's eyebrows went up. "It seems I heard something about a leopard."

"Well, I guess I was rescued, sorta," Johnny admitted lamely.

"I guess you were!" Rick paused, looking at Johnny. "You sure don't sound very friendly."

"I don't like thieves and traitors," Johnny said defiantly.

"Wait a minute!" Rick began.

At that moment the four hunters entered the room, cutting off the rest of Rick's sentence. The scarred-faced leader spoke to Rick.

"You know you're not allowed in here. Get out!" His voice was low and threatening. Rick turned to go.

"Hold it," called Barney, the narrow-faced hunter. "Carry this in to the kitchen." He dropped a haunch of antelope on the floor.

His face set and calm, Rick walked slowly past Johnny and hoisted the meat to his shoulder.

"Any other orders?" he asked quietly.

"Yep!" Ed said. "Take the kid with you. Rustle him up clothes of some kind. Then you can put him to work helping you."

"Come on, Johnny." Rick put his hand on Johnny's shoulder and started for the door. Johnny followed him, shrugging off the friendly hand.

The kitchen was even neater than the main room. As soon as they entered the room, Rick tossed the haunch of antelope into the sink. He turned, faced Johnny, and grasped the boy's shoulders with his big freckled hands. He seemed angry.

"What's this thieves-and-traitors business mean?" he demanded.

"First you pretended to be on our side," Johnny answered, "and then you let the rhinosaurs get in, so those hunters could steal our marva claws."

"So that's what you think," Rick said. He regarded Johnny gravely. "Does the rest of the colony think that, too?"

Johnny nodded.

"Take a good look at me, Johnny." Rick touched a cloth tied around his middle like an apron. "I'm cook and housekeeper here, not one of the gang. I wasn't pretending anything, and I didn't let any rhinosaurs inside. I came with these outlaws because they had their tank guns leveled on me."

"But why did they do that?" Johnny demanded.

"Harkness' orders," Rick replied. "Remember his threat?"

"I sure do!" Johnny said. His eyes grew wide. "I was right," he went on. "I thought Mr. Harkness was the boss those hunters called."

"He sure is the boss," Rick said. "He's given out word he'll pay for any information about you and Baba. Any information he gets he passes on to this bunch. The gang has to work for him so he'll market their stolen claws and arrange their passage to Earth. Why he's even offering to pay double for Baba just to prevent the colony from getting him."

"Golly!" Johnny breathed. "He really must be sore at us." Johnny sat down on a kitchen stool. It was cold against his bare bottom. He looked up at Rick. "Gosh. I'm sorry, Rick. I mean about thinking you were, uh, well, you know."

"That's all right, Johnny." Rick was smiling now. "I admit it did look bad. Let's forget it and get you into some clothes. We have a meal to fix."

Johnny jumped up. With a friend beside him things didn't seem quite as bad. Helped by a pair of scissors, Rick soon had him into a pair of cut down trousers and a baggy shirt. As soon as the clothes were on, the two started preparing the meal.

As they worked, Johnny questioned Rick about what had happened to him. Outside of beating him up once, the hunters hadn't treated him too badly. He was being saved for Trader Harkness. They made Rick stay in the kitchen and wouldn't let him into the main room except to clean it up, and then kept a gun on him. The gang kept him from escaping by a very simple means; they locked up the rhinosaur-hide armor in a closet. Ed kept the closet keys, as well as the keys to the tank and helicopter, fastened to his wrist. Rick had been watching carefully but had not seen one chance to escape.

As Johnny served the meal to the outlaw hunters, he looked the room over carefully. When the men weren't looking, he clicked a greeting to the little scarlet ape. It immediately became quite excited. A plan for escape began to shape itself in Johnny's mind. He said nothing to Rick, however.

After the outlaws had eaten, Johnny and Rick had their meal. Rick thought it strange, but Johnny couldn't bring himself to eat any of the antelope; he remembered all too well the tiny antelope leader he had held in his hand. When they were finished and had washed the dishes, Johnny was all too glad for a blanket thrown on the kitchen floor; the same kind of bed Rick had.

Johnny tried to push away his fears for Baba, but it was a long time before he could get to sleep.

It seemed only minutes later when he was rudely awakened by a rough blow on his shoulder. Actually it was ten hours later, as he could see by the clock above the stove. Johnny reared up to see Ed standing over him, a smile on his thin lips, his pale eyes jubilant.

"Get up and get your clothes on," he ordered. "We're going places."

Johnny jumped up and reached for the baggy clothes Rick had made him.

"Come on in when you're ready and don't waste any time about it," Ed directed, and strode back into the other room. Johnny slipped on the pants and was soon stuffing in the shirttails of the oversized shirt. Rick stood by the stove and watched, sympathy in his eyes.

"Baba," he said slowly, "arrived at the colony an hour ago. I was listening at the door when the call came from Harkness. These guys are planning—"

"Come on!" Ed stuck his head in through the door and cut Rick off. Numb with worry, Johnny followed Ed into the main room.

"Better wrap him up in something," the outlaw called Barney said, his narrow face twisted in a strange grin. "We can't let the arrow-birds get him now."

Johnny stood while they strapped man-sized armor on him and put a helmet on his head. He followed Ed out of the door and into the helicopter. The outlaw leader seated Johnny beside him, switched on the motor, and they roared away.

"Where are we going?" Johnny asked.

"You'll find out," Ed snapped. "Keep quiet till I tell you to talk!"

They flew on for almost an hour. Then Ed set the helicopter controls on automatic hover and snapped the radio telephone on. He dialed a number. Johnny saw that the number was that of Colony Headquarters.

"Hello." Ed made his voice high and nasal. "I have information concerning Johnny Watson. Let me speak to his father."

The slick-haired blond man put his hand over the telephone mouthpiece. He grabbed Johnny by the collar and stared directly into his eyes.

"Listen," he said, "when your father comes on, I want you to speak to him. Tell him you were rescued by us and we've treated you O.K. Understand?"

Johnny nodded, his mouth dry.

"I'll tell him what happened," Johnny said. He didn't understand why Ed was making such a fuss about it.

"Hello. Hello. This is Frederick Watson." Johnny was thrilled by the sound of his father's voice over the telephone.

"Hello, Mr. Watson," Ed said in the fake voice. "We've found your boy and here he is." Ed handed Johnny the telephone, his hand over the mouthpiece again. "Remember!" he said in a threatening voice.

"Hello, Dad!" Johnny said into the telephone. "I'm safe all right."

"Thank God!" his father's voice replied.

"I was rescued by these men and outside of making me wash dishes and sleep on the floor, they've treated me fine. I'm—"

Ed took the telephone away from him in mid-sentence.

"But where are you, Johnny?" Johnny could still hear his father's voice.

"Right now," Ed said into the telephone, "Johnny's up in a 'copter. You needn't try to get a direction finder on us. Rescuing this boy cost us a lot and we gotta be sure you'll pay us for it."

"I offered a reward." Mr. Watson's voice was anxious.

"It ain't enough," Ed said. "We lost a tank and a 'copter getting him. He was surrounded by rhinosaurs. We have the boy. You've got a live marva. I figure it should be a trade. You bring the marva to the old tank road by the river, and we'll bring the boy. Bring one tank, driven by one man. That's all. Be there forty-eight hours from now. Do as I say and the boy will be delivered on schedule."

"Hello, hello." Frederick Watson's voice was frantic. "I don't know if the colony will—" Ed hung up and snapped off the radio.

"They will," he said.

Johnny's spirits had never been so low. Everything he touched seemed to turn to disaster. The colony was all but ruined. In trying to protect Baba he had caused the marshberries to be destroyed and had given these outlaws a chance to steal the colony's marva claws. By running away with Baba he hadn't saved the little bear at all. The outlaws, Trader Harkness' outlaws, were going to get him. Johnny would not only lose Baba, but the colony, too, would lose its last chance for survival.

XIII. Outwitting the Outlaws

The little red monkey screamed and chattered its hate as Johnny and Ed stepped through the doorway of the cabin after their eventful flight. Johnny had noted that the cabin door was the only exit.

As was usual on Venus, the exit was a double door. When the outer door was open, the inner one could not be opened. It was just like the school door. If Johnny could once get through the outer door and block it open, it would be a while before the men could break the lock on the inner door and get out. Getting out the first door would be the problem; but not too big a problem. The outlaws didn't think that he could go into the jungle without armor, so they did not watch him or the door too carefully.

As soon as they were inside, Ed took off Johnny's oversized armor and locked it away. He then winked at the other men and sat Johnny down in front of him on a high stool.

"You know who I am?" Ed asked him.

"Sure," Johnny said. "You're Ed."

The big man cuffed him so hard he fell from the stool.

"Boy," he said, "you never saw me before." He frowned, making his scarred face as evil as he could. "When you go back to that colony, you're going to forget you ever saw us. Do you know why?"

From the floor Johnny shook his head.

"Because if you tell anybody our names or anything about us, you know what we're going to do?" Ed asked.

Again Johnny shook his head.

"We'll catch you and take you out into the jungle and tie you to a tree without any armor on, and leave you for the arrow-birds. You understand?"

Johnny nodded his head. They thought they were scaring him.

115

They talked a little while longer, describing things they might do to him if he told their names, and Johnny pretended to be afraid.

"All right," Ed said after the lecture. "Get back to the kitchen."

"Can I play with your monkey?" Johnny asked.

"Play with that monkey!" Ed's pale eyebrows went up. "He'd chew an ear off you. I've been trying to tame him for a month; and he don't do anything but bite. You leave him alone."

"He won't bite me," Johnny said. "I don't think he will." The monkey would be a big help in escaping, if only they'd let Johnny get close to him. "I'll just go get some sugar cubes from the kitchen."

"Let him, Ed. It'll teach the brat a lesson," the narrow-faced Barney put in.

"O.K." Ed said. "Get bit, if you want to."

Johnny rushed through the open door into the kitchen. Rick was sitting at the table with a book beside him.

"You got any candy, Rick?" Johnny asked. "Or maybe some sugar cubes?"

"You better not fool with that monk, Johnny," Rick said. "He's plenty mean, like all the Venus creatures."

"He won't hurt me," Johnny said. He saw a box of sugar cubes in the cupboard and grabbed it. "Monkeys just love sweets."

"No." Rick leaned over and a big freckled hand closed around Johnny's small brown one. He took the box of sugar away. "I'm going to tell them you got scared. Only two things will happen if you try playing with that monk. You'll get bitten, and they'll get a big laugh."

"Please let me, Rick," Johnny said. He paused a minute and whispered, "I've got an idea how I can get away."

"What!" Rick exploded. He closed the door and went on in a whisper, "It's impossible. You haven't any armor. You don't have any weapons or a tank. Don't be silly." He paused, and looked at Johnny. "Well, how were you going to do it?"

"Simple," said Johnny. "First I make friends with the monkey. Then I'll let him go and tell him to run around and jump on Ed and the rest. While they are chasing him, I'll open the inside door. I'll let him out first and dive through myself. I'll wedge open the outside door, and by the time they get their armor on and break the lock on the inside door, I'll be over the wall and gone." The words tumbled out of him.

Rick shook his head. "Johnny, that week in the jungle has gone straight to your head. In the first place, how are you going to make friends with the monkey? Then how are you going to tell him anything? And how are you going to get any armor?"

"Rick," Johnny said, "I don't need any armor."

"Oh, Johnny!" Rick exclaimed, exasperated.

"They just won't bother me." Johnny took a deep breath. "I can talk to them, same as I can talk to the monkey!"

"What!"

"Now, listen, Rick," Johnny whispered earnestly, "I wasn't hurt when I came here, was I? I'd been in the jungle six Earth days without any armor."

Rick was looking at him with a strange expression.

"Do you remember," Johnny went on, "how I looked when you rescued me from the rhinosaur?"

Rick nodded.

"Did I have any armor on then?"

Rick stared at Johnny for a few seconds.

"By golly!" His mouth was slightly open in amazement. "You didn't have any armor on!"

"I wasn't hurt, was I?"

Rick shook his head slowly.

"No," he said, "but what about that leopard and the rhinosaur?"

"The leopard wasn't hurting me," Johnny said. "She was trying to get me away before the men got me. She was my friend. As for the rhinosaur; well, Baba and me hadn't learned for sure about them, yet."

"But how can you talk to them?" Rick asked in wonder.

Johnny knew he had no choice; he had to trust Rick completely.

"It was Baba," Johnny said. Then, very quickly, he explained about Baba's clicks, and told Rick about his three secrets.

"Jeb said something about those clicks one time," Rick said thoughtfully. "I never dreamed it could be true."

"It is true, though," Johnny insisted.

Ed stuck his scarred face through the doorway.

"Well, kid, getting cold feet about the monk?"

"No, sir!" Johnny said. "Rick was just getting me some cube sugar."

"Well, hurry it up." Ed went back out.

"Johnny," Rick said, "you show me with that monk, and by the moons of Saturn, I'll come with you, armor or no armor!"

Johnny was bewildered. This was something he hadn't counted on. He wanted to explain that there was a chance even he, alone, could not succeed without Baba. Just as Johnny started to speak, Ed appeared in the doorway again.

"Well?" he said in his heavy voice.

Johnny took the sugar cubes from Rick and followed Ed into the main room. As he always did, the monkey screamed and chattered at them as they entered. The little animal was chained to its perch. A spring catch too strong for its tiny fingers fastened the chain to its collar and kept it from getting away. The outlaws began to gather around.

"You'll have to stay at the table, way over at the other end of the room," Johnny said to the men. "He's scared of you." He pointed to the table, which was as far as possible from the door leading outside.

"All right, all right." The four men seated themselves where Johnny pointed, ready to watch the fun.

Johnny walked slowly up to the tiny monkey. As he did so, its little red face twisted and it showed its razor-sharp fangs. It screamed at him. Then it leaped out, only to be jerked back cruelly as it came to the end of its chain. But it ran out as far as it could and clawed at Johnny, its eyes red.

"Friend-pet, friend-pet," Johnny clicked very low in the back of his throat. The animal stopped screaming and cocked his head at him. It looked from one side to the other, as if looking for a marva behind Johnny. Johnny repeated the phrase again and again, holding the sugar out where the red monkey could see it and smell it.

Johnny didn't have any idea how much the little animal could understand, but he went on clicking. "I'm your friend. We are going to get away from these men." He repeated this many times. Then he remembered that Rick was going to try, too. "You and I and the big man in the other room are going to escape."

As Johnny talked, he moved forward. Soon he was well in range of the little monkey's nails. It jumped forward. Johnny put a sugar cube in its paws. With a gurgle of pleasure, the monkey swallowed the sugar and put out its paw for more.

"Jump on my shoulder," Johnny clicked. The little creature regarded him silently. Then, with a graceful hop, it was on his shoulder.

"I don't believe it," Ed's voice rumbled.

As soon as the hunter outlaw spoke, the little monkey growled and bared his teeth at him. The man muttered something under his breath, angry that a small boy had done what he couldn't do. He started out toward them, and was quickly in range of the creature's teeth.

"You'd better not," Johnny said. "He'll—"

The monkey dived at Ed, his teeth slicing into the man's shoulder. The outlaw jumped back, cursing. Blood ran down his shirt.

"I'm sorry, Ed," Johnny said. "Let me work with him just a little while, and maybe he'll make friends with you, too." In his anger the man had picked up a heavy stick to hit the monkey. The other men broke into laughter.

Ed grunted something, and threw his stick at the men who were laughing. "Come on," he said, "let's play cards." Johnny turned back to the monkey.

For almost half an hour Johnny talked to the monkey in the marva clicking language while the outlaws played cards across the room. He guessed the little animal could understand a little more than the mother leopard could. That wasn't too much, but it was enough. He made the creature understand that when he was released, he was to fly at the men. He wasn't to hurt them, but make them chase him until Johnny could get the door open. Then the monkey was to leap for the opening. The hardest job was getting the monkey to understand that he shouldn't harm Rick if the ex-bodyguard came with them. Johnny wasn't sure the monkey understood.

With his back turned to the outlaws, Johnny undid the collar about the monkey's throat. Keeping the little animal out of their sight he walked toward the exit door. He picked up an old boot to use on the outer door.

"Hey," Ed suddenly shouted, "where's the monk?"

"After them," Johnny clicked. The monkey leaped at the oncoming Ed. He clawed his face, then leaped at the other men. He made great jumps by swinging from light fixtures by his long black tail. Ed wheeled and charged like a bull after the tiny screaming creature.

"The kid let the crazy thing loose!" he shouted. "Catch it!"

"Shoot him!" yelled Shorty, drawing his blaster pistol from its holster. Ed knocked it from his hand, and it went sliding along the floor.

"Want to kill us, too, you fool?"

In the excitement Johnny worked the latch on the exit door, and pressed the button that opened it. He saw Rick half way through the kitchen door. Rick reached down and grabbed up something from the floor. The monkey was jumping from head to head among the yelling outlaws. Not one of them noticed what Johnny was doing.

The door was open. Johnny nodded his head toward Rick, who came at a dead run. When Rick was almost there, Johnny clicked as loud as he could, "Come, friend-pet! Come!"

In one leap the little animal sailed across the room and landed on his shoulder. Johnny and Rick pushed through the door, slammed it behind them, and opened the outside door.

Johnny paused a second and wedged the boot he had picked up into the outer door. The outside door could not close and the safety lock would keep the inner door closed.

"Come on, Johnny," Rick shouted. "This way!" He rushed through the helicopter landing space toward the tank entrance. Rick pulled the switch that opened the duro-steel door.

"Dive for the nearest tree trunk," Rick shouted. "They have gun mounts on the roof."

Johnny ran after Rick, his short legs unable to keep up with the older man. The little monkey was riding on top of his head, shrieking and chattering. As soon as they reached the forest the monkey jumped into a tree.

Johnny stopped dead. He needed that monkey. The little animal could tell other animals he and Rick were friendly.

"Friend-pet monkey, friend-pet monkey," he clicked, "come with me." For an instant he was afraid the animal had not heard. Then, with a shock, he felt it drop down on his head.

"Rick, Rick," he yelled, "stay with me." With relief he heard the big man coming back. "You gotta stay with me," Johnny panted. "Arrow-birds." Rick nodded, and ran along beside Johnny.

They ran among the great pillars of the diamond-wood forest until Johnny thought his breath would come no more. His feet were heavy against the springing leaves; his legs began to twist with fatigue. When he was about to fall, Rick whisked him up in his arms.

The little monkey screamed and jumped at Rick's head.

"No, no!" Johnny clicked. The tiny creature jumped back on Johnny's head, but he had left red claw marks on Rick's face.

Far in the distance they heard the noise of a tank motor starting. The diamond-wood trees were beginning to thin out. Soon they would be in the jungle of meat trees which always surrounded a grove of the giant trees. The sound of a helicopter motor starting up was added to the sound of the tank. The noise of the tank motor lessened. The outlaws had headed in the wrong direction. The helicopter was the great danger now. Hiding under a meat tree, with its heavy leaves, was their best chance.

"We'd better get under something, Rick," Johnny said. His breath had returned. "Let me down."

Rick nodded. His breath was coming in great gasps. A heavily leafed tree surrounded by brush was a few hundred yards ahead of them. Johnny pointed to it and Rick nodded. Johnny prayed that there were no arrow-birds feeding there. This close to the hunters' lodge there shouldn't be many animals, but arrow-birds were always on the watch.

As they worked through the brush to get under the meat tree, Johnny really missed Baba. The first branches were too high for either Johnny or Rick to reach. If Baba had been there they could have easily climbed up into the protection of the tree's leaves and branches. Luckily the brush was high and thick around it, screening them from view from the side. The tree itself screened off the sky.

Once they had reached the trunk of the tree, they stood wordlessly for a while, breathing hard.

"Any idea where we are, Rick?" Johnny asked in a whisper.

Rick's big, bony face broke into a smile. He reached into a pocket. Out came a small map of the Venus continent.

"Not for sure," he said. "But we can't be far from the lodge." He pointed to a mark on the map. "Once we see the lay of the land, we should be able to tell." Suddenly Rick froze stone still. Johnny looked up.

An arrow-bird had flown into the tree. Since its head was not in position to strike, it was probably looking for a meat fruit. Just as Johnny saw it, its head turned toward them.

Johnny clicked out a sharp command for it to leave them alone.

As the little purple eyes sought them out, its head snapped into striking position. But as Johnny clicked on, it moved its head back to a friendlier position. Its little purple eyes stared directly at them.

Rick regarded Johnny with wonder.

"I don't know what that little bear taught you, but it sure is a miracle," he said. He then reached into his shirt. "I'm still glad I got this. Did you see Ed knock it out of Shorty's hand?" He pulled a blaster pistol out of the shirt.

As soon as the gun came out, the red ape leaped from Johnny's head, screaming. The arrow-bird snapped its head into position to strike.

"Drop it, Rick! Drop it!" Johnny yelled.

Amazement swept over Rick's face.

"But why—"

125

"Bother us not, friend-pet," Johnny clicked loudly. At the same time he knocked the blaster from Rick's hand.

He was too late.

The arrow-bird shot with a sickening smack into Rick's shoulder. Almost as quickly it withdrew its blood-stained beak and was hovering in the air for another strike.

XIV. Captured!

Rick stood rigid, his face twisting with pain, a hand clutching his upper arm. The greenish bird hovered in the air, its wings a blur of motion.

"We are friends. We are friends. Bother us not, friend-pet!" Johnny clicked deep in his throat. The bird continued to hover, its little purple eyes darting back and forth from Johnny to the wounded Rick. Its bloody head stayed in arrow position, but it drifted farther away.

Johnny remembered that when he had had an arrow-bird on his shoulder, the others had left him alone. He dreaded changing his command, but he did.

"Come to your friend," he clicked firmly. The arrow-bird stared at him distrustfully, but came closer. The monkey dropped back on Johnny's head. With a sigh of relief, Johnny saw the arrow-bird's head snap out of attack position. He put out his hand and the arrow-bird lit on it.

"Are you hurt bad, Rick?" he asked. The words made the arrow-bird flutter with alarm, but Johnny soothed it by petting it with his other hand.

"Not too bad," he said through clenched teeth. "The thing seemed to dodge when you made that clicking noise."

"I'm sorry, Rick," Johnny said. "You just shouldn't have shown that gun; you'll have to leave it behind. If they think you'd harm any of them, they'll kill you, just like that. The monkeys almost got me 'cause of a pocket knife."

"I didn't know," Rick said. He looked at the bird on Johnny's shoulder. "Seems peaceful enough now."

"You better let him sit on your shoulder, Rick." Johnny looked down at the arrow-bird and stroked it again. When it was quiet he placed it on Rick's shoulder. The man was nervous and the bird was worried, but they both did as they were told.

They waited under the tree while the helicopter went back and forth above them. Johnny looked at Rick's wound. It didn't look too serious, but Johnny knew better than to count on that. The slightest arrow-bird wound could be deadly if not treated. Johnny had seen hunters brought into the colony sick from an untreated scratch. They should have brought an emergency kit, but the kits were only carried in special pockets of the armor.

They let Rick's wound bleed to cleanse it as much as possible. Then Johnny bound the arm tightly and made a sling for it from a piece of Rick's shirt. Rick gave Johnny his wrist watch to wear, since his wrist was hidden by the sling. After that they waited. It seemed the helicopter would never go away. Once it hovered almost directly above them, but then went on.

While they waited Johnny looked over the map. The outlaw hideout was not as far from the colony as he had feared. They had to start soon and make good time, but they just might be able to make it to the meeting place the outlaws had set before Johnny's father got there. There was a fighting chance if Rick didn't get too sick. Finally they heard the sound of the helicopter landing far in the distance. Taking direction from the map, they set out on their way. Rick's wound was less painful now, but Johnny kept his eye on his red-haired friend. They started out at a fast clip, following an animal track which led in the direction they wanted to go.

In a few hours of steady marching they were a safe distance from the outlaw hideout. Johnny's idea was working out. Several flights of arrow-birds had passed them by with no more than a glance in their direction. One flight had hovered above them while the arrow-bird on Rick's shoulder twittered and shrieked to them. Then they had flown off at top speed. A troop of monkeys had also let them pass without doing them any harm. Hundreds of the small red apes had followed along beside them for some time. Johnny's monkey chattered to them from his perch on the boy's head. Then they, too, had swung off through the trees at top speed. Rick had been awed, for he had never seen Venus animals so close except when they were attacking.

At first Rick's strides had been long and Johnny had had to run every few steps to keep up. Now Rick's steps were short and slow. He seemed to be getting weaker and weaker. They had stopped and cleaned his wound again at a spring and rebound it, but he was not doing well. The big red-haired man was pale under his freckles; his lips were set tight.

Johnny kept close beside him as they moved forward. They had worked out a path to follow that skirted diamond-wood groves and avoided rivers. It was too easy to become lost in the dense forest, and Johnny was very unsure of what river snakes would do.

Suddenly Rick stumbled. He stopped and balanced himself by leaning on Johnny's shoulder. He looked at Johnny with bloodshot eyes, sighed and crumpled up on the ground. The arrow-bird that had been sitting on his shoulder hovered in the air above him making little squeaking noises. He flew toward Johnny and then down an animal trail that led off toward a diamond-wood grove. As Johnny leaned over to look at Rick the monkey jumped from Johnny's head.

Johnny stared down at Rick Saunders' face. His cheeks were flushed but the rest of his face was grey. The little monkey sniffed the wounded man and chattered something at Johnny. Then he, too, ran down the side trail. When Johnny paid no attention, he came up to Johnny and plucked his sleeve, chattering all the while. Johnny looked around. He thought the monkey was drawing his attention to some antelope berries growing down the path. Johnny clicked to the little red monkey to gather some. When the red monkey returned, clutching a cluster of the large berries in each tiny paw, Johnny took them and squeezed the clear red juice into Rick's mouth.

The man coughed and turned his face away. But gradually his eyes opened. They were dull and feverish. His hand went to his shoulder and he winced. In the few hours that had passed, his arm and shoulder had already swollen a great deal. He raised his head. Johnny helped him to his feet, but when he staggered, Johnny helped him lie down again on a patch of grass by the antelope berry bush.

"I can't go any farther, Johnny." Rick's voice was hoarse. "Those birds must have some kind of poison on their beaks. That wound feels like it's on fire."

"It's not poison, Rick," Johnny explained. "They eat the meat fruit and little pieces stick to their beaks. The pieces get rotten and infect wounds bad." Johnny remembered that Rick was a Terran and had been on Venus barely a year.

"There's only one thing to do," Johnny went on. "I'll have to light a signal fire with lots of smoke. Somebody will see us then."

Rick shook his head slowly. "No, Johnny, it won't do. If those hunters come they'll get you again and they're likely to finish me off. You take the map and go on…" Rick's voice trailed away. He struggled to sit up.

Johnny stepped forward, wondering what was wrong. The monkey leaped off his head and bounded into a tree. Slowly Rick raised his good arm and pointed directly behind Johnny.

Johnny turned. Staring at him through a bush was a coal black saber-toothed leopard, crouched to spring.

"Friend-pet, go away!" Johnny clicked in the marva tongue. Oh, if Baba were only here! The monkey chattered from a tree.

"Go away! Go away!" Johnny repeated. Then he saw a second leopard. A third. None of them was his friend, the mother leopard. These leopards stood almost a foot higher and were solid black. Their saber fangs were a full foot long. These were deadly males, hunting in a pack.

The one behind the bush gave a coughing growl. All three slinked slowly toward Johnny and Rick on silent feet, their mouths half open, their white teeth shining.

"Go away, bother us not! Friend-pets, bother us not!" Johnny repeated. The leopards moved smoothly forward, their steel-like muscles rippling under the shining black fur.

Frantically, Johnny turned to Rick, who was struggling to his feet.

"They won't obey, Rick!"

"Run, Johnny," Rick said. "Run for a tree!" Rick thrust the boy behind him, but Johnny would not leave his friend. Rick turned, pulling Johnny, and started to run.

At the same moment a leopard sprang through the air, high over their heads. A split second later he was in front of them, barring their way, his gold eyes glistening, his fanged mouth giving forth a low growl. The growl meant, "Come."

Johnny looked about. Not four steps away was another of the lion-sized cats. They were ringed around by the creatures. Johnny tried clicking again, but they paid no attention.

"My arm, Johnny!" Rick groaned. He ran his hand over a forehead which was dripping sweat. Slowly his legs gave way and he fell in a heap beside Johnny. The leopards moved closer, their mouths wide. The one in front was getting so close that Johnny could feel its breath blowing against his bare arm.

Then it moved too fast for Johnny to follow. Johnny felt the great jaws close around his middle, and he was

133

hurled off his feet. Frantically he beat at the big head. The jaws tightened, gripping him painfully. As Johnny cried out in pain he saw the other two leopards leap upon Rick.

A few seconds later Johnny was being carried down the path in the jaws of the monster cat. The jaws had tightened no more than was necessary to hold him firmly as the animal trotted along. From this strange position Johnny witnessed an even stranger sight. Behind the leopard carrying Johnny strode the two others. Side by side they walked, dividing Rick Saunders' weight between them. One had its jaws about Rick's arms and shoulders; the other held his hips and legs. They moved along easily, their heads held high so that his feet would not drag on the ground.

Then Johnny saw that his arrow-bird friend was riding on the shoulder of one of the leopards that was carrying Rick. He heard a chattering noise, and knew that the little red monkey was close by.

The leopards were taking them some place, but who could know where? In his odd position Johnny could not tell even the direction they were going. But soon they were in the patchwork shadow of a meat tree forest. Here the leopards had their lairs. But they did not stop. They went on and on. Johnny kept trying to watch the leopards which carried Rick. Once in a while he could catch a glimpse of them, Rick's head bobbing as they moved. He was still unconscious.

Then Johnny heard a shout and a scuffling noise. The leopard carrying him turned around. Rick was conscious. His head was turning about wildly and he was yelling. His eyes lit on Johnny.

"What's happening?" he all but screamed.

"They're taking us somewhere," Johnny answered. "They haven't hurt me yet."

Rick was kicking his feet and struggling, making it hard for the leopards to walk. Johnny could see their jaws tightening as Rick struggled.

"You better not fight, Rick," Johnny said. "You can't get away and they'll just hurt you more. I'll tell them you won't fight if they'll hold you easier." He clicked the message to the big cats. His own leopard turned back up the trail, and he couldn't see what the other leopards did. A few seconds later he heard Rick's voice.

"You were right, Johnny. When I eased up they eased up, too." Then he laughed in a strained way. "I wish they'd eat us right now and get it over with."

"Maybe they won't."

They said no more. They were coming to the edge of the meat tree grove. As was often the case, the last group of meat trees was beside a river. Beyond was a diamond-wood grove. The three animals plunged into the cool water, and soon were swimming, with Johnny's and Rick's heads held well above the water. On the opposite bank they dived into the shadow of the diamond-wood grove.

As soon as they entered the grove Johnny was startled to see that there were several antelope walking beside them. Then, suddenly, the little red monkey he had rescued from Ed was squatting on the leopard's back. Johnny heard a swishing sound almost under his head. By twisting hard he could see the ground. There was a river snake crawling beside them. Its ugly horned head was right beneath him. It was the first time he had ever seen one.

Then his heart leaped.

He heard the clicking of the marva language. Johnny twisted his body against the leopard's teeth, trying to see where the clicking was coming from. The leopard growled, and Johnny lay still again.

"Take the big killer to the healer," the voice clicked. "The little killer take to the council." The clicks were somehow different from Baba's, firmer and louder; but Johnny could understand them perfectly.

Johnny caught sight of the two leopards carrying Rick. They were turning down another path. The river snake and the antelope took the same path. But Johnny's leopard went on forward. After a short time the leopard stopped and very carefully opened its jaws and eased Johnny to the ground. It turned and walked a few steps away. There it crouched.

Johnny got slowly to his feet. The little red monkey jumped on his head. The arrow-bird perched on his shoulder. In a clearing among the diamond-wood trees Johnny stood in the center of a circle of jewel bears, their blue nails glowing in the half-light. All but one or two were dark about the muzzle. They sat on their haunches, staring straight at Johnny.

XV. A City in the Trees

Except for faint animal sounds in the distance, there was silence in the diamond-wood grove. More marva than any other person had ever seen surrounded Johnny. Most of them were dark muzzled and very old. From old Jeb's hunting tales Johnny knew that as a marva grows older the fur about its muzzle darkens. A jewel bear with a black muzzle was a rare thing. This was no ordinary group of marva, but a gathering of elders. They seemed neither friendly nor unfriendly. They seemed to be waiting patiently for Johnny to do something.

"Hello," Johnny broke the silence, greeting them in their own clicking language. "I am very glad to see you." Once started, Johnny had so much to say the words fairly rushed from him. "Your leopards sure scared us. Maybe you can tell me how to get to some people quick. Before it knew we wouldn't hurt it, this arrow-bird wounded my friend and he's very sick. And Baba's got caught again, and some bad men are trying to get him. If you could help us get back to the colony, oh, I'd thank you! Baba's a marva, you know, just like you and he's my best friend. We tried to find you, but the outlaws captured me and Baba went home because I'm his friend-pet-brother and he thought I'd be there. Rick will die if you—"

The torrent of words was cut short by a marva with a coal black muzzle. He stood up and raised both furry blue paws for silence.

"It was well reported that the little killer can speak our language," he clicked, with a sound very like a human chuckle. "You speak well," he clicked to Johnny, "but you speak too much at once." A ripple of amusement passed over the faces of the jewel bears. Then they became stern once more.

"You must try to tell a little at a time," the old marva continued. "But first, let me answer one of your questions, for I think you are full of questions. The red-furred killer has been sent to the healers. He will soon be treated. We heard of you and of the wound from our friend-pets. You need not worry, little killer. Our healers have had many wounds to deal with since your kind has been in the green lands."

"You mean you will fix up my friend?" Johnny asked. "You have doctors?"

"Yes, little killer," the black muzzled one answered.

"But he won't understand," Johnny said. "He wouldn't let any of you touch him – not unless I talk to him."

"Follow the leopard, then. He will take you to the healers. Then return here." The black muzzled marva waved his paw and the leopard rose and trotted off. Johnny ran beside him.

In another clearing Johnny paused in amazement. It was filled with many animals. He saw several rhinosaurs with great gaping blaster wounds. A leopard with a cut on its shoulder lay whimpering before a marva, who was squeezing the juice of some berries upon the cut. Fascinated, Johnny watched as the marva sewed up the cut with a fine piece of marva claw for his needle. The berry's juice must have killed the pain for the leopard stopped whimpering and lay very still.

Then Johnny saw Rick. He was lying on his back, but his eyes were open. The two leopards were right beside him, their heavy paws holding him down.

"Rick!" Johnny called, running up to him.

"Get away from here," Rick yelled. "There's a horned snake right beside me. He'll kill us!"

"No," Johnny answered. "If he'd wanted to, he could have done it long ago. Rick, we're safe! The leopards brought you here to get your wound fixed up." Then he clicked to the leopards, "Let him go. He won't run away." He turned back to Rick. "I just told the leopards you won't run away," he explained. "Just watch the marva over there."

Unsteadily, Rick got to his feet. He quickly sat down again, overcome by weakness and amazement. He had caught sight of the marva healers at work. One was sewing up a rhinosaur. Another was splinting up the leg of an antelope. Rick shook his head.

"I'm dreaming," he said. "I must be!"

"Isn't it wonderful?" Johnny said. "They're going to fix your wound, too."

The leopard beside him growled, in the way Johnny knew meant "come."

"I gotta go now," Johnny said. "Goodbye, and don't worry. Let them do what they want to."

Johnny and the leopard made their way among the sick animals. Johnny let out a cry of pleasure. There was his friend the leopardess. The blaster burn was not a bad one, and it had already been treated. She rose when she saw him. Though the big male leopard growled his disapproval, Johnny ran over and patted her and her cubs before he went on.

"Is she a friend of yours?" Johnny was startled by the sudden appearance of the black muzzled marva who had spoken to him earlier.

"Yes, old one," Johnny answered respectfully.

"Come!" the marva addressed the leopardess.

The two leopards, the cubs, Johnny and the marva walked off together. Soon Johnny was in the circle of marva again. This time he was over his surprise and he tried to tell his story as clearly as he could. He was beginning to get worried about the time that was passing, and he looked at Rick's watch again and again. There was always the chance that the outlaws would try to get Baba, even though they no longer had Johnny to give in return. But he told his story as best he could.

In spite of his worry, he had to explain all about men on Venus. He even had to tell where men came from, since the jewel bears had never seen stars or planets in their sky. He told about overcrowded Earth and his father's desire to make a colony. He told about the hunters and Trader Harkness. He told about his trip into the jungle and how the outlaws had captured him, and, finally, of his escape with Rick into the jungle.

The group of marva listened carefully. Sometimes they nodded their heads in approval of what he had done, and sometimes they seemed puzzled. But they seemed more friendly when he had finished.

When at last he came to a halt, the old marva who was acting as spokesman for the group arose.

"You say this young marva friend of yours is named Baba?" The old one used the word in the clicking language for Baba's name.

"Yes."

"We have heard of him," the black muzzled marva clicked, "though he was not of our grove. His mother and brother were killed. We have wondered why he was not killed too, since your people feel we are your enemies. Our observer on Council Rock has watched your people often, but has seen little we can understand. Tell us why Baba was not killed at first."

"I already explained," Johnny said. "His teeth and claws were black. Now they are blue and, of course, he's worth a lot of money."

"What is this money?" the black muzzled one asked.

Johnny was surprised. The word Baba used for money must not be a real marva word. If only Baba was here to explain! Johnny tried the best he could to explain how money works. The marva shook its head in wonder at the strange ways of men.

"But why do you want our claws and teeth?" the marva asked.

"To make rings and plastic." But they understood neither the word "ring" nor the word "plastic." Johnny had to explain that plastic was the material that helmets were made from. He explained also that rings and jewelry were used for decoration.

"And that is why we are killed on sight?" asked the marva.

"Yes, old one." It made Johnny sad for himself, for the marva, and for his people, to have to admit this.

His answer caused a stir among the marva.

"I have one more question," the old marva said. "Why did you come into the jungle with the marva, Baba?"

"He would have died or been killed otherwise, and he was my brother, or like my brother. It was like the song he sang:

"You help your friends
And your friends help you.
It is the law
And will be the law as the trees stand.
Between friend and friend there is no parting
More than the fingers of a hand."

"We know the song," the marva said, gently. "But didn't you think these" the marva gestured at the leopards, "might kill you?"

"Yes," Johnny said, "but I had to take the chance."

They asked many more questions about men and their ways. Many were hard for Johnny to answer or even to understand, but he tried very hard to be as clear and truthful as possible. Finally they seemed satisfied, and there was again silence in the diamond-wood grove.

With a nod to Johnny the black muzzled marva led the rest of the jewel bears away, and left Johnny and his animal friends alone. A short distance away the marva again formed a circle and clicked together quietly.

Then they called over his friends: the leopardess, the red monkey, and the arrow-bird. They appeared to be asking them questions. Johnny, left to himself, wondered what was happening. It was all very strange. Rick's wrist watch said too much time had passed already.

The black muzzled marva returned to Johnny.

"Come with me," he clicked, and walked toward one of the great trees. One of the younger jewel bears waited at the foot of the tree. "Grasp him by the shoulders," the black muzzled marva directed Johnny, "and hold tight." Johnny found he could ride easily on his back. The marva started up the tree at a breathtaking speed. The full grown marva climbed three times as fast as Baba could without anything on his back. Down below them the black muzzled marva followed with the slow dignity of age. Up and up they went, the full two hundred feet toward the sky. Johnny looked down at the sick animals and the healers. They looked very small now.

Finally Johnny and the marva reached the branches. As they came up to the first huge branch, it appeared to move slowly away from the trunk of the tree, to reveal a large opening. The tip of the branch was fastened to a branch above. Two huge snakes the color of the branch were coiled about it. These snakes had pulled the branch from the opening so that the marva and Johnny could enter. Johnny could see that the branch had been hollowed out until it was fairly light.

Once inside, Johnny's eyes were dazzled by light. The young marva started back down the tree. In a few moments the black muzzled marva was before Johnny again. He made a little bow.

"Man child," he clicked, "welcome to the tree of Keetack, leader of the council of this grove. May you have long life."

"Thank you." It was the only thing Johnny could think of to say.

Before him was a beautiful room. There were finely woven grass mats upon the floor, and in places about the room piles of mats of soft blue and delicate pinks made places to sit. The room was flooded with light that came from directly over their heads. The walls were made of the living wood of the tree carved with many scenes of Venus and colored to make beautiful designs.

Johnny looked up to see where the light came from. He gasped.

Above them was a great cluster of marva teeth and claws, glowing with light. When Keetack, the leader of the council, moved forward, the light floated along the ceiling following him. Finally, Johnny realized what the light was. It was a cluster of the large Venus fireflies. Each clasped a marva claw in its tiny feet. As the insect glowed, the claw multiplied the light. In the middle of the ceiling was a hive where the fireflies lived. Johnny watched with wonder as the flies went back and forth from hive to light.

Keetack noticed Johnny's interest. "As one becomes tired," he said, "another takes his place. We give them food and they give us light. Is it not a good system?"

Suddenly Johnny understood. "And the rhinosaurs protect you from the sea beasts…"

"And we help them when they are sick or hurt. We help take care of their marshberries and see that they have food. All living things are our friends but the killers of the sea."

"Gee," said Johnny, "it's just perfect."

The little bear appeared to laugh.

"Hardly," he clicked. "We have our quarrels too, and many of our friends sometimes forget."

"That's right," Johnny said. "The monkeys sure didn't trust those leopards until after we got here."

"It is hard for many of them," Keetack went on. "I often wonder what the rhinosaurs will do when there is nothing left to fight. We are already beginning to make friends with the killers of the sea. Not long ago the arrow-birds were killers, and it was only in the lifetime of my great grandfather's great great grandfather's father that we made friends with the river snakes, so that they, too, do as we advise them to do."

"You mean obey you?" Johnny asked.

"In a way," Keetack answered, "most of the animals obey us."

"But they don't obey your little ones!" Johnny was excited. "It's only when your blue teeth come in and your voice gets deep that other animals will obey you. Isn't that right?"

"Yes," said Keetack. "We say a deep voice is a sign of the coming of wisdom."

"Then that's why the arrow-birds obeyed Baba and me?"

"Yes," Keetack nodded. "Now would you like to see the remainder of our tree?"

"Please," Johnny answered politely. "It's a lot like the caves in New Plymouth Rock."

"Indeed so," said the marva leader. "Those caves served as a yearly meeting place of the Council of All The Groves. No one tree was large enough for all to live in while we talked together. Before your people came to the green lands we had happy times there each year. Now we use the rock only for watching you."

"I'm sorry," Johnny said.

"Come now," Keetack clicked. "I will show you the tree."

Johnny would have been terribly excited by the suggestion if it hadn't been for his fear that they were taking too much time.

The whole upper part of the tree was honeycombed with rooms. Each level was connected by a winding passage as in the caverns of New Plymouth Rock. Each was lit in the same way. It was not Keetack's tree alone; several marva families lived there together. As they entered each level a marva would come forward and welcome Johnny. He was fascinated by the little ones, who grinned at him just as Baba did.

The marva cubs always came in twos: peeking around from the back of the mothers were always two pairs of bright blue eyes. But one family was different. Johnny and Keetack entered that level to the sound of growling and tumbling and scratching. In the middle of the room a small bear bounced hard on the floor and up to the ceiling where it clung like a fly. Below it a coal black leopard cub growled in a way Johnny understood. It was a pleading growl saying "Come."

As soon as the baby bear hanging on the ceiling saw Johnny and Keetack he dropped to the floor and stood with his arm around the black leopard cub. A mother marva came rushing from another room.

"I'm sorry my cubs were so rude," she clicked, "but you know how much mischief one of ours and a friend-pet-brother can get into."

"Of course," Keetack clicked. "This is the friend-pet-brother of one of ours, so he will understand."

"Oh, yes!" Johnny said. Then he looked over at the two cubs. The little marva was still very small and had black claws. "He shows off just like Baba used to," Johnny exclaimed. Johnny remembered the trouble his mother had had with Baba's game of walking on the ceiling.

With that they went on, but Johnny touched Keetack on the shoulder. Though the bear was old, he came no more than to Johnny's shoulder.

"The leopard cub was that marva cub's friend-pet-brother – just as Baba is mine?" Johnny asked.

For the first time the marva seemed to smile, opening his mouth wide as Baba did when he grinned.

"We would say you were his friend-pet-brother," the black muzzled one clicked. "Perhaps it is better to say you are friend-brothers. It is not strange. Many of us have had companions of another race."

"But why is this?" Johnny asked eagerly.

"You have seen that our cubs always come in pairs. The pair is almost one until they are grown," Keetack explained. "If only one cub is born, or one of a pair dies, we give the lone cub a friend-pet, a cub of another race to grow up with him. They become brothers just as you and Baba did. Without this the lone cub would die. Cubs need the love of a brother as much as they need food. It is sometimes a very good thing, for in this way our friends of the plains and the groves are knitted to us with ties of very deep love."

"Now I understand why Baba would never leave me," Johnny said. And then he went on earnestly, "And you should understand why I've got to get back to Baba in the colony. There may still be some way I can save him. But I don't have much more time."

"I can make no promise yet to let you go," Keetack said. "Still there may be a way we can save your friend-brother and do something more besides." He would say no more.

Soon they were back in Keetack's rooms.

"You will wait here," Keetack said.

Johnny seated himself on one of the piles of mats and waited. He didn't quite understand what was going on, but he wished Keetack would hurry. He looked at Rick's watch. It had been twelve hours since he had spoken to his father on Ed's radio telephone. He had only an Earth day and a half to get to the settlement if he were to keep Baba out of Ed's hands.

A few minutes later Keetack reentered the room, surrounded by some of the furry bears who lived in his tree. "My friend," he clicked, "I have a gift from the people of my tree to your people – those whom you say are making a colony. It is a gift of friendship and a gift of peace. If the Council of the Grove decides to let you go back, I hope you can use these to pay for the life of your friend and brother, Baba." In his hand the marva held a small package wrapped with woven rushes.

"Thank you," Johnny said, and took the package.

"You may unwrap it."

Johnny folded back the stiff material, and gasped. In his hand glowed a pile of marva claws – hundreds of them!

XVI. The Thunder of Rhinosaur Hooves

A worried Johnny was standing in the center of the clearing once more, surrounded by the little jewel bears. He now knew this was the grove council, a group of the wisest bears of the grove. Keetack's gift to Johnny had impressed them all. They knew it meant that Keetack trusted Johnny. Yet they were cautious. Johnny's knowledge of them could be very dangerous.

"It is not right he should go," one of the marva was saying. His muzzle was still blue, and Johnny knew this meant he was younger than the rest. "The young killer will return to his people and tell of our ways and of our houses in the trees. Then the older killers will come with their death-spitting things and our lives will be gone. I think that we should hold him here. Otherwise we risk the lives of our people."

Johnny put up his hand as if he were in school. The marva, Keetack, of the deep black muzzle, pointed at Johnny.

"May I talk now?" Johnny asked. The marva nodded. "I won't tell anything you don't want me to," he promised earnestly. "With these claws I'm sure Baba can be saved, but I'm going to have to hurry. If the outlaws get him they will kill him sure. Don't you understand?"

"We understand," the old marva answered. "But we must be sure of safety for us and our people. Your people are killers like the beasts of the sea. You even kill each other. You are a strange people. Still you risked your life for your friend Baba, just as Baba would risk his. Your friend with the red fur risked his life to help you. Do you really think that if your people knew all there is to know about us, they would not come with the fire spitting things?"

Johnny was silent. He knew Ed would come. He knew Trader Harkness would, too. He swallowed, for lying to these little bears was something he just couldn't do.

"For those claws some of my people would do anything," he clicked in a low voice.

There was complete silence in the grove.

The marva who was young and still blue furred about the muzzle stood again. Johnny wanted to cry. He had condemned Baba to death, but if he hadn't done so, maybe all the marva would be killed. He felt they, too, were his brothers. He broke into sobs and stood there with tears running down his cheeks.

"We have heard our young friend," the blue-furred marva said. It was the first time he had not called Johnny a killer. "He gave us the truth because we have trusted him, and treated him with friendship. I was wrong. He is to be trusted. Let him go from here with his gifts. My tree, too, will send a gift. But let him promise to keep secret anything he thinks may be dangerous to us." The marva seated himself.

"Oh, I promise," Johnny said solemnly. "Cross my heart and hope to die."

"It is agreed among us then?" Keetack asked the group. The furry heads nodded their agreement. "Young friend, you may go. Your settlement is three groves away from us. You may have a rhinosaur to ride. It will take you home with time to spare. You go with a pledge of peace. We will send messages ahead and no animals will attack you. Nor will any of our friends attack any man unless he attacks first. You may tell your people we will give them more claws for such things as we would like from them. Every two years we marva get a new set of claws and teeth. The old ones have been saved from generation to generation to be used for lights and for tools. You may also tell the leaders of your people we would like to meet with them. Perhaps we can make a friendship that will endure!"

Johnny had a busy hour ahead of him. First he ran to see Rick among the sick animals in the other part of the grove. There was no question of Rick's coming with him. He was still too sick from the arrow-bird's wound, but he was definitely on the mend. He was lying under a tree, petting the leopard cubs. Johnny told him what had happened, carefully omitting where the marva lived, and Rick became more and more interested. Finally Johnny showed him one of the packets of claws that he had been given. By now the packets had grown to over a dozen, and he had placed them in a bag made from his shirt.

"Johnny," Rick said, "you've done a most wonderful thing! Those marva don't have to worry about being hunted any more. If people can get so many of those claws and teeth, no one will ever want to hunt for them again. You tell them that, for me."

Johnny rushed to give the news to the marva. The first one he found was the young council member who had at first opposed letting him go.

"It pays to trust one another," the marva said simply.

Soon Johnny was ready. The leader of the council brought before him a huge rhinosaur, one of the biggest Johnny had ever seen.

"Skorkin knows he must obey you," Keetack said. "He will do anything you ask, and will harm none of your people."

"Hello, friend-pet," Johnny said.

The rhinosaur turned and looked at him with his little blue-black eyes and grunted a greeting. Johnny noted it. It probably meant "hello."

"Was that his speech?" Johnny asked.

"Yes," Keetack answered. "They have more words than the other creatures of the green lands. Only the monkeys of all our friend-pets come near to being as smart as they. They are a people, too, of great courage."

"I know," Johnny said. He remembered the rhinosaur charge at the colony.

At the mention of the word "monkey," the little red ape whom Johnny had rescued from Ed began to chatter and jump up and down.

"He likes you and wishes to go with you," Keetack said. "Do you want him to?"

"Oh, yes," Johnny answered. The monkey leaped to his shoulder. Johnny suddenly had an idea. "Could the leopardess, her cubs, and the arrow-bird come too?" he asked. "That is, if they want to?"

Keetack understood what was in Johnny's mind and nodded his approval. "It is a good idea," he clicked. "It would be a good way to prove to your people that the animals can be friendly."

The leopardess was suddenly beside Johnny, rubbing up against him like a big cat. She looked up into his face and growled in the way that Johnny knew meant "come."

Johnny looked at the wrist watch. "We do have to hurry."

He threw the bagful of the precious claws over his shoulder, and stepped toward the rhinosaur. "How am I going to get on?" he asked, with sudden surprise.

A series of grunts came from the rhinosaur, that sounded something like laughter. Then it lay its horned snout upon the ground, and grunted again.

"Climb on," Keetack said.

Grasping one of the long snout horns, Johnny climbed aboard his strange mount.

"Goodbye," he shouted. All around hundreds of the marva were hanging from their trees. They waved and he waved back. "Let's go!" he clicked to the rhinosaur.

And so began the race through the jungle. The great rhinosaur moved forward with thundering speed, the leopardess and her cubs loping along beside them. When one of the cubs grew tired it leaped on to the rhinosaur's back, curled up beside Johnny and went peacefully to sleep. The arrow-bird perched on one of the beast's horns and the monkey beside it. They did not stop for rain or rivers. Everywhere the jungle seemed to have blossomed forth with animals, who waved and grunted, growled, clicked, or sang greetings to them as they went past.

The broad back of the rhinosaur was a perfect place to travel, Johnny found. It swayed hardly as much as a helicopter and bounced much less than a tank. It was not long until Johnny had followed the leopard cub's example. He found a hollow in the big back, curled up and went to sleep, lulled by the steady swinging movement and the thunder of the rhinosaur's hooves.

Johnny woke with a start. The monkey was pulling on one of his ears; they had reached the settlement. Johnny glanced down at his watch. He had slept six hours.

The rhinosaur had stopped right at the edge of the meat tree grove that bordered the settlement. Through the screen of trees Johnny could see the high grey walls. It was about half a mile to the gate. Johnny wiped the sleep out of his eyes and puzzled as to the best way of making his appearance.

"Go that way," Johnny clicked, and pointed. "But stay where you can't be seen from the walls." At a slow trot, the rhinosaur carried them to a place directly in front of the gate to the settlement wall. Johnny saw that the gate had been repaired. Beside it was a steel door through which a single man could be admitted.

"You wait here for me," he said to the animals. "Let me down, friend rhinosaur." He tied his bag of claws to the rhinosaur's horn and then walked down the huge head to the ground. The arrow-bird flew over and lit on his shoulder. It had not understood. "Wait," Johnny repeated. "Wait, I will come back."

The rhinosaur wandered a few yards away and began to munch on some bushes. The leopard growled to her cubs and began to climb a meat tree in search of food. Johnny smiled. They were good friends to have.

Johnny slipped through the bushes and trees until only one antelope berry bush was between him and the wall. The guard tower was directly in front of him. The men in the tower must have noticed the swaying of the bushes, for they were looking directly toward the spot where Johnny stood.

Johnny slipped from behind the bush and stepped into full view. He smiled and waved jauntily to the guards. As casually as he could he started toward the door. Halfway there he began to skip for sheer joy. The guards were staring at him open-mouthed. Obviously he had no armor on. He had had to use his shirt to make the bag for the claws. The only clothes he wore was the baggy pair of shorts Rick had made him.

The steel door at the base of the guard tower opened at his touch. He closed it carefully, opened the inner door and then climbed the stairs to the guard tower, instead of going straight into the colony. There, too, were double doors.

"Hello," he said, as he entered.

The three guards on duty were so surprised they couldn't speak for a second. One of them was Old Jeb. Before they recovered, Johnny went up to Jeb. "Would you call my father, Jeb, and tell him to come to the gate?" It was funny to watch their faces.

"Johnny, you're safe!" Jeb suddenly exploded. He swept the boy into his arms and swung him about. He stopped, pushed the boy away from him, and tousled his hair. "I can't believe it, but you're safe!"

"Sure am," Johnny said, with a grin. Then he became serious. "How is Baba? Is he all right?"

"He's been kind of sad and upset, poor little feller," Jeb said. "But how in thunder did you get here? Last we heard you were being held for ransom. Your folks have been worried sick."

"Oh, I got away from the outlaws and some friends brought me. Please call everybody in the colony, will you? Tell them to come to the gate. I have something important to show them. I've got to go back out to my friends now. Bye." He started toward the door.

"Friends! What friends?" Jeb called.

"You'll find out," Johnny said, with a laugh.

"Hey, you can't go outside without armor," one of the other guards shouted. But Johnny had slipped out before he could be stopped. He took the stairs at a run, and was out of the heavy steel wall doors before the men could follow him.

As he skipped across the open space back to the jungle, he turned his head, waved to the men in the tower, and smiled.

"Come back here, you little devil!" Jeb shouted through the loudspeaker the guards used to guide tanks in.

But Johnny shook his head and went back into the brush.

Johnny waited for about ten minutes. All this time the loudspeaker in the tower was shouting for Johnny to come back in. Finally the voice changed. It was Johnny's father's voice.

"Johnny," his father said over the speaker. "Come on in here! Please! I'm here now. Johnny!"

Johnny heard a tank starting up inside. He didn't want any tanks coming after him.

"Come on, friends," he clicked to the animals. He climbed back up on the rhinosaur's back. The leopard came running up with her cubs. The arrow-bird and the monkey, taking no chances, followed behind them, leaped to their usual perch – the top of Johnny's head.

"Let's go!" Johnny clicked to the rhinosaur. "Walk very slowly out toward the big black place."

Johnny clicked to one of the cubs to jump up on the rhinosaur's back beside him. Johnny crawled to the broad head of the rhinosaur between two of its horns. The leopard cub sat on its haunches beside him. The mother leopard and the other cub ran alongside them. The rhinosaur's hooves made muffled thunder as he walked.

A big grin on his face, and waving his hand, Johnny emerged from the jungle into full sight of his father, Jeb, and many others inside the guard tower.

"Stop when we get a little way from the door," Johnny said to the rhinosaur. The big beast grunted its understanding.

Johnny and his friends came to a halt close enough to the tower so that Johnny's voice could be heard.

"Open the gate, please," Johnny shouted. "We want to come inside." He saw his father's startled face above him. "Hello, Dad. How's Mom? Did she worry too much?"

"Hello, son." His father's voice was shocked. "Your mother is all right." He paused. "Where did you... How did you...?"

"You mean the animals?" Johnny asked, rather enjoying the effect he was making. "Oh, they're friends of mine. You can let us in. They won't hurt anybody. I'm bringing a present to pay for Baba and make up for all the harm we did. Look." He took a packet of the claws and opened it. He let a handful of the claws run out of one hand into the other in a shining blue waterfall. Through the microphone he could hear his father and the other men gasp.

"Come in here quick," Frederick Watson's voice came back over the loudspeaker.

"Open the gates, please," Johnny repeated.

"But the rhinosaur! And the leopard!"

"They're friends of mine. They brought me here. They won't hurt anybody. I promise."

The big steel gate slowly opened. Riding on the back of one of the greatly feared rhinosaurs, Johnny entered the colony.

It seemed that everyone in the colony had heard of Johnny's strange return. Pioneers – men, women and children, hunters and guards – were hurrying toward the big gate. At the sight of the rhinosaur, a woman screamed and the crowd ran, scattering in all directions.

Captain Thompson, two other colonists and a hunter held their ground, their blaster pistols out.

"Don't shoot! Don't shoot!" Johnny shouted. Beneath him the rhinosaur trembled. "He won't hurt you. He's our friend." He stroked the arrow-bird on his shoulder. "Look! Even an arrow-bird!"

Slowly the blasters that had been leveled at them were lowered. Hesitantly, one or two of the people began to move back toward the little group.

A woman came running toward Johnny. It was his mother. Tears were running down her face. Even she was finally stopped by the bewildering sight of her son surrounded by jungle animals.

"Let me down," Johnny clicked to the rhinosaur. The big animal lowered his head. A cry went up from the people as the leopardess bounded after him. Johnny threw his arms about his mother.

"Oh, Johnny, Johnny!" his mother said over and over, holding him tight against her armor. She stiffened as the mother leopard rubbed against them and the arrow-bird lit, for a moment, on her shoulder.

"Mother, I want you to meet my friends," Johnny said. "This is Mona, the leopardess, and her two cubs, Pat and Mike. And this is Skimpy, the monkey. I haven't named my arrow-bird yet." Then he spoke to the animals. "This is my mother."

Johnny's mother stood there a moment, too bewildered to speak. The leopardess licked her hand. Then Johnny led his mother to the rhinosaur.

"This is my friend Skorkin, the rhinosaur. He gave me a ride all the way here. Isn't he beautiful?" Then he clicked to the rhinosaur, "This is my mother."

The huge creature grunted.

"Skorkin said 'hello,'" Johnny said.

Her eyes wide with the strangeness of it all, Johnny's mother nodded a wordless greeting to the creature.

Just then Johnny heard a sound he had been waiting for. It was the sound of a basketball dropped from a height. He looked up to see Baba bounding along as fast as he could come. Johnny was off at a dead run to meet him, leaving his mother and the other animals behind.

The two of them met at top speed, and they met with such impact that both were tumbled to the ground in a heap of arms, legs, boy and bear. Both of them were laughing when they got to their feet.

"Oh, Baba, you bad little bear!" Johnny said. "I thought I'd never see you again!"

"And I!" Baba said.

"You shouldn't have come back here!" Johnny said. "I'll have to punish you right now!" He grabbed Baba suddenly by the leg, whirled him around and around above his head and threw him as high as he could in the air. Throwing his arms around as if frightened to death, the little bear whimpered and clicked. But just before he hit the ground he made himself into a ball, and bounced higher than Johnny had thrown him. Then, on the third bounce, he landed lightly on Johnny's shoulder.

Their delight was cut short by the sight of a fat bald man who glittered as he walked toward the crowd. For an instant Johnny was afraid. It was Trader Harkness. Then he remembered – the trader's days of power were over.

"Mr. Harkness," he called, "I've got something to show you."

"They said you had claws." The trader's little black eyes fixed their gaze on Johnny.

"Come on, I'll show everybody."

The crowd parted for Johnny and Baba and the trader. By this time almost all the colonists and visiting hunters were gathered around the rhinosaur and the leopards. A few bold souls were timidly petting the cubs. Probably of most interest was the arrow-bird. Tired from all its riding, it had put its head under its wing and gone fast asleep, perched on the rhinosaur's horn.

Johnny took the bag he had made from the shirt down from where it hung beside the arrow-bird. He untied it, revealing the many packets made from woven rushes. Packet after packet, he spilled the claws out on to the shirt until there was a great pile of jewels glowing before the people.

"Where did you get them?" Trader Harkness' voice rumbled. He was shocked and pale.

"The marva themselves gave them to me for the colony," Johnny replied. "It's a sign that they and all the animals want to be our friends."

The trader forced his eyes away from the pile of jewels and looked over his shoulder. Johnny was suddenly conscious of three hunters standing behind the trader. Ed and his gang!

"I'll take those claws now," the trader said. The gang whipped out their blasters and leveled them at Johnny and Baba.

The crowd gasped and then fell silent. Johnny's father stepped up, but one of the hunters waved him back with his gun. Johnny saw he'd been wrong. There was plenty of fight left in the trader. He glanced around him; the animals had become very still, waiting his word.

"Friends," Johnny clicked, "stay still. This man is a killer."

Skorkin, the rhinosaur, snorted. The arrow-bird awoke and snapped its head into arrow position. The monkey bared its teeth, while Mona, the leopardess, crouched to spring, the muscles of her haunches trembling.

Johnny saw the trader's eyes widen. The leopard was not three feet away from him. Thinking fast, Johnny stepped carefully over and put a hand on the leopard's shoulder.

"I wouldn't move, Mr. Harkness," Johnny said, his voice quavering in spite of himself. "If you don't tell your gang to give their guns to Captain Thompson, I'll tell the animals to charge. Maybe Ed told you what I made the monkey do?" Johnny's heart raced. It was a bluff. He couldn't tell the animals to charge. He knew they might be killed. No amount of claws would be worth that.

The trader's eyes were fixed on Mona. Then Skorkin snorted again, eager to fight.

The trader turned brick red. "Do what the kid says," he said in a low, strangled voice. The blaster in Ed's hand wavered and then came down.

There was a deep sigh of relief from the crowd.

Grimly and quietly, Captain Thompson gathered up the guns. "All right, you men," he said, "there's a room ready for you at the stockade."

The fight was really gone from the trader now. His shoulders slumped, his head down, he shuffled as he was led away.

Johnny's father stepped forward and embraced him.

"I don't understand how you did it, Johnny," he said. "I don't understand anything about it. But this is certainly a wonderful day!"

XVII. Teachers Can't Play Hooky

It was now an hour after the Earth rocket had blasted off on its way back to Earth. Johnny Watson lay on his stomach with his chin cupped in his hands and looked down from the top of New Plymouth Rock. Beside him, twisted into the same position, was his friend Baba, his blue nails glowing in Venus' pearly light. Near the two friends, perched on a boulder, were two of the large Venus eagles, watching every move they made.

How changed it all was down in the settlement! People were streaming back from the rocket field on foot and without armor. Beside the Jenkins family strode Mona, the leopardess, carrying a basket in her mouth. In the basket the Jenkins' baby slept. Mona just loved babies. Down in the marshberry fields three rhinosaurs peacefully browsed. There were so many berries available now in the sea marshes that no one had to worry about the few in the fields. The marva had left these three rhinosaurs to carry people wherever they might want to go.

High in the sky was a faint dot. Baba nudged Johnny and pointed.

"Here comes Keetack," he said in his clicking language. "We'll have to go down pretty soon."

"I suppose so," Johnny said wearily.

It had been fun for a while being the only person who understood the marva language. When Dad and the other colonists had gone into the jungle to talk with the council of all the marva groves, Johnny and Baba had been there too. They were the center of attention. When the men spoke, Baba told the marva what they meant. When the marva spoke, Johnny had to tell the men what the bears meant. It had been fun being so important. It had been fun being treated like heroes, but they were already tired of it. With their new freedom to travel, there was a whole continent to explore, and hundreds of new friends to make.

Idly, Johnny watched the dot, that Baba said was Keetack, grow into a bird with a twenty-foot wing spread flying through the sky. In its claws was a small black-muzzled bouncing bear. Baba's eyes were magically good. The bird was a Venus eagle; and the marva's airplane. Before men had come and made it dangerous for them, the marva had flown anywhere they wanted to go in the talons of these great birds. Johnny knew that the earliest hunters thought the eagles were preying upon the bears. It was just one more surprising thing about the little bears. Johnny remembered what Rick had said when he had arrived home, his wound all healed. He had really grown to respect the marva.

"They have learned to live with other creatures, and have taught all their friends, as they call the animals, to live in peace together. The meat eaters have their meat trees so they don't need to attack other animals. It's amazing," Rick reported.

Johnny remembered how Baba had preened himself when Rick had spoken that way, and he smiled.

"Hey, Baba," Johnny said, "how soon do you think we could take a trip all around the groves? We could get Skorkin to carry us, and go visit everybody."

"You will have to come stay with my people," Baba said. Only a few days before Baba had discovered a host of aunts, uncles and cousins in one of the outlying groves. Most important of all he had found his father. "I've lived with you for years and years. Now it should be your turn."

"Oh, good," said Johnny. "We'll do it, soon as they'll let us go."

"Look, Johnny," Baba pointed. "Look at the trader!"

Below, the fat bald-headed little man, a pack on his back, was heading into the jungle. He waddled as he walked, but he moved straight along.

"Where's he going?" Baba asked.

"Dad says he's going to start a marshberry farm if the marva will let him. But, gosh, it'll be a long time before anyone will help him."

"He can always live on meat fruit and stuff," Baba said. "Nobody likes him, but they won't bother him if he leaves them alone."

What had happened to the trader and to the outlaws was the strangest thing of all. The marva had not wanted them punished. They said they wanted to make friends, not enemies.

The thousands of marva claws that had been given to the colony had made the claws quite cheap, so that Trader Harkness had become a poor man. He had been rich in hunting equipment and hunting lodges and now all these things were valueless. Surprisingly, he had refused to return to Earth.

"Venus is my home," he had said flatly. "I'll get by."

Johnny had to admire his courage, just as he had to admire some of the hunters who would not stay on Venus. These lean hard-bitten men were going further on into space.

To Johnny's surprise Keetack admired the hunters, too. "They are fighters, like the rhinosaurs. Here there is nothing left to fight. They are people of much courage."

Looking down on the trader, Johnny found he couldn't help feeling sorry for him.

"Goodbye," he yelled, his voice echoing among the rocks. "Goodbye, Trader."

The fat man looked up and waved back. Johnny thought he smiled.

"He was a real pioneer," Johnny said.

"Yes," Baba answered, "he'll be all right."

Johnny jumped back suddenly from the edge of the rock and hid behind some bushes. "Here comes Mom, looking for us!"

Baba quickly dived back out of sight too.

Johnny peeked through the screening of bushes. His mother was riding toward the rock on Skorkin, the rhinosaur! This hideout was not very secret. Everybody on Venus knew about it. He stood up, and waved down to her.

"I'm coming, Mother," he shouted.

His mother nodded and the big rhinosaur turned back toward the settlement.

In a few minutes Baba and Johnny would be back in school, sitting in front of a group of men and a group of marva. Baba would be teaching the marva how to understand the talk of people, while Johnny taught the men and women how to talk and understand the language of the marva. It was a hard job.

"I guess we gotta go back!" Johnny mourned.

"I guess so!" Baba agreed sadly.

"There is only one trouble with being a teacher," said Johnny. "Teachers just can't play hooky." Then he grinned. "Say, I've got an idea!"

"What?" asked Baba.

"Mom hasn't been doing her homework. Let's give a test today!"

Baba slapped his furry haunches, his blue teeth glowing.

"Let's go!" Johnny clicked to the two eagles. He ran as hard as he could and leaped off the edge of the high cliff, hurtling down and down. Right after him, Baba jumped, too.

There was the sound of great wings, and the two tremendous Venus eagles swept after them. One dived at Johnny, its claws spread. The long powerful claws hooked into Johnny's belt and whisked him through the air toward the settlement. The other grasped Baba by the shoulders. Together the two friends flew on.

"That was fun!" said Johnny.

His furry blue pal nodded his agreement.

Publisher's Afterword

As far as I can remember, I have always loved reading. My mother said I taught myself to read when I was two and, perhaps because she was a teacher, she encouraged this start by supporting what would become a lifelong habit.

One of my favorite childhood books was a science fiction story about a young colonist on Venus and his sentient bear friend that I checked out from a local library. For years as an adult I have vainly tried to obtain a nice copy of my own to share with my children. Finally, I decided to publish it myself. I am proud that the very first book published by Terran Press™ should be Venus Boy.

For the most part, this story is as Lee Sutton wrote it in the 1950s. However, I have edited the book to correct a few errors that made it into the original work and to make it friendlier for modern readers. For example, I substituted the word *helmets* every time Lee used *headglobes*. The intent was to keep as much as the original content as possible without making the reader stop and ask what did the author mean by a certain word or phrase. The revised edition also includes more art than the original novel.

This version was created with the encouragement and help of two families. I am very thankful to the Sutton family for their permission and encouragement for making Lee's masterpiece available to another generation of readers. They also shared an original illustration that has never before been available to the public. The following image was an early drawing of a Venusian saber-tooth leopard.

You can see that the trees appear differently than the ones in the book. One can only imagine the discussions between the artist and the author as the illustrations were being developed. The original drawing was given to Lee Sutton by Richard Floethe and is used with the permission of the Sutton family. All rights to it are reserved by the Suttons.

All of the other illustrations are the intellectual property of the art estate of Richard Floethe. I appreciate the Floethe brothers for their work in maintaining the art of their father and for authorizing the use of his unique illustrations – including two others they had saved that were not in the original novel – in this version. One of them gives us another glimpse of the Venusian forest along with the ever vigilant arrow-birds.

This may be the forest that Johnny and Baba brave in Chapter 10, although Johnny had neither his helmet nor armor during the time in the forest covered by the book. So we can imagine that this illustration captures some of Johnny's earlier adventures with Baba. The final newly unveiled drawing is another perspective of the activity described in Chapter 7. It is the first tank illustration in this revised version. More information about the art and life of Richard Floethe is available at a website created by one of his sons (http://richardfloethe.com).

For a book written in the 1950s – before Sputnik, the lunar landings, personal computers, cell phones, and the digital revolution – the book is remarkably timeless. While Johnny's adventure could obviously never happen on Venus given what we have learned since the 1950s, it is fun to think that it may be possible on a future colony in another solar system. I hope the story brings you and your loved ones as much pleasure as the original story brought me.

Lance Gentry

Made in United States
North Haven, CT
10 June 2024

53457101R00104